My Husband

Rumena Bužarovska

MY HUSBAND

Translated from the Macedonian by Paul Filev

DALKEY ARCHIVE PRESS
McLean, IL / Dublin

Originally published in Macedonian by Blesok as *Mojot Maž* in 2014.

Copyright © by Rumena Bužarovska, 2019.

Translation © by Paul Filev, 2019.

First edition, 2019.

Library of Congress Control Number: 2019951869

Dalkey Archive Press
McLean, IL / Dublin

Co-funded by the
Creative Europe Programme
of the European Union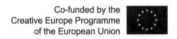

Printed on permanent/durable acid-free paper.
www.dalkeyarchive.com

Acknowledgements

Since initially appearing in Macedonian in 2014, some of these stories have been edited, which accounts for the slight differences from the original publication.

I would like to extend my deepest gratitude to Steve Bradbury, Vivian Eden and Matt Jones for their valuable contribution in editing the translation of these stories.

Rumena Bužarovska

Contents

My Husband

Rumena Bužarovska

My Husband, the Poet

I MET GORAN at a poetry festival. He'd started going gray. His hair is now almost completely white. I think he's convinced it's part of his "new sex appeal," as he once told me. He tried to make it sound like a joke, but I think he actually meant it. I felt like asking him whether he thought thinning hair and a scalp the texture of melted wax were part of that appeal, but I kept my mouth shut. He can't take criticism. He blows his lid and sulks for days. Then I have to do something to butter him up, such as "randomly" quoting a line from one of his poems.

The other day he got really pissed when I didn't want to read what he'd written the night before.

"I don't have the time right now," I said. "Tomorrow."

"You don't have the time for three poems?" I could sense the anger in the rising pitch of his voice, but I knew that, whatever I said, he'd take it the wrong way, so I didn't say another word.

"Go on then," he said, "hit the books," and slammed the door. He always says that whenever I have to prepare a history lesson. It's his way of saying that, if I really knew my subject, I wouldn't need to prepare. "If you know your stuff, then you know your stuff," he'll add, smugly.

To be honest, I don't like reading his poems, much less having to listen to them—something he makes me endure betimes. When we were still in love and before the kids came along, we'd have sex and then he'd whisper a few lines in my ear as I lay there panting and sweaty on the bed. They were always about flowers—mainly orchids, because they remind him of pussies—about southern breezes, about oceans and seas. He'd also mention exotic spices and fabrics, like cinnamon and velvet. Something about my tasting like cinnamon, my skin feeling like velvet, my hair smelling like the sea. Which I know isn't true, because my mother once told me my hair stinks. Anyway, at such moments his words used to excite me. I would get all aroused and feel like making love again. Although if he couldn't get it up right away, I'd have to repeat the lines to stay aroused until he could.

He doesn't do that anymore, thank God. I've gotten so sick of his poems that I don't want to read another line, let alone listen to him recite one. Even though I'm forced to do the second of these every now and then, otherwise, as I said, he gets really pissed, and I don't like to subject myself or the kids to conflict. It's been ever since we stopped making love very often that he's started reciting them aloud, standing in the middle of the living room, beneath the bright ceiling light, which accentuates his bulbous nose and oily complexion. That's when I realized his poems aren't really all that good and more often than not they're simply about the fact that he writes poetry. The idea seriously excites him. Sexually, I think.

Take this one, for example:

She has the scent
of autumn
like drops of rain
streaming from the eyes
my words
turn her into my poem

It may not be the best example, but it's the only one I know by heart, the one I quote lest he blow his lid. I'll hum "my words / turn her into my poem," which he finds really flattering because he's always wanted someone to set his poems to music. He doesn't realize it would be impossible. His poems don't scan and they make no sense. Empty phrases cobbled together, which to the ordinary person might sound like God knows what when they stumble on an exotic word like "cinnamon" or "velvet." As they did to me when I was young and stupid and susceptible to such tricks.

God, was I stupid. I just can't forgive myself for it. Anyway, I was recounting how we met at a poetry festival. I was there as an interpreter, because before I started teaching history, I did some interpreting on the side to earn extra cash. One night, in the lobby of the big hotel where the poets and interpreters were staying, we all got together and sang folk songs. Now I know how all those small-time poets love to put on a big show, as if to say, "Not only do I know how to write poetry, not only am I a sensitive soul, but also I understand traditional music, on top of which I'm a good singer." That's when Goran made his appearance. In keeping with the occasion, he was wearing a white shirt embroidered with traditional motifs. Actually, he looked really good. Goran was very handsome. To be honest, that was the main reason I fell in love with him. He had a muscular chest and strong, hairy arms—arms that you wanted always to hold you, never to let you go, to carry you away. Anyway, unlike the others, Goran wasn't sitting, but standing, leaning against a wall, observing it all with his head cocked to one side. Then came a moment when everyone fell silent. He straightened up and sang a folk song. I'm positive it was *More, sokol pije—Behold, the Falcon Drinks—* because I now know that it's the only one he knows. He belted it out, theatrically, his eyes closed, his head thrown back, his Adam's apple bobbing up and down. He looked like a rooster crowing. He looked funny, but at the same time I couldn't stop myself staring at his arms and his chest, imagining him carrying me off somewhere. When he stopped crowing, he won a round of applause and looked straight at me. His eyes were a little teary—probably from the effort of belting out the song—but at the time they seemed filled with sorrow. I felt a powerful urge to comfort him. And that is what I did, later the same night, in his room, and that's how it all began.

He still goes to poetry festivals. He goes every chance he gets, whenever he can get time off work, which he sucks at, by the way. I can just imagine what's he like at those festivals. To start with, he takes a suitcase full of those scrawny little books of his poetry, with their badly laminated covers. He's had most of them translated into English, as well as a number of Balkan languages, so that others can read his drivel. Since I don't speak any of the languages that interest him, by some miracle I haven't been forced to translate any of his poems. Not that he thinks I'd be any good at translating poetry anyway. According to him, I don't know how to appreciate it because, obviously, I haven't shown much interest in his work lately. The translations are terrible. Not in terms of the content—his poems are meaningless anyway—but because they're poorly worded and full of grammatical errors. That's because he's so cheap. He wants his poems translated, but he won't pay to get it done properly. So he always finds some poor young thing, whom he probably seduces with his hoary "sex appeal," to translate his work either free of charge or for next to nothing. A few times I've overheard him discussing the arrangement with them, offering as recompense, say, ten copies of his book. It's just so embarrassing, but what can I do?

When he comes back from these poetry festivals, he shows me the photos on his digital camera. He always gives it to someone else to take photos of him. He has a load of them showing him reciting a poem at a podium, holding a microphone or one of his crappy little books. He wears the exact same expression in every photo—"Ah, your poetry face," I'll say to him, which for some reason he finds flattering. His brows are knitted, one higher than the other, as if he were both troubled and touched. His chest is thrust out, his hair freshly washed, fluttering in the spring breeze of those seaside towns where they hold the festivals he's particularly fond of attending. The other photos are mostly of women, rarely of men. The festival volunteers—the young women—they don't concern me. I doubt they'd fancy him anyway. He's too old and foolish. Nowadays he attracts a different type of woman. The distinguished lady, a bit on the plump side, flabby around the waist and under her arms, where the fat bulges out the sides of her bra. She always wears a tight red or black blouse. Occasionally she sports a big floppy hat. Her hair is dyed black. She wears red lipstick. Cheap, flashy jewelry adorns her fat little fingers and big fat neck. She wishes to radiate a version of mature femininity, an aura of mystery, and to taste like cinnamon, to have a voice like velvet. Let her try. Maybe Goran can help her. I really couldn't care less.

But sometimes at night he'll snuggle up close and whisper, "Open, my orchid," and I do.

Soup

I GET UP in the morning and stare at the pot in which he used to boil his water. Next to the jar of brown sugar is his box of green tea. I open the box. There are only three teabags left. I'll finish them, I think to myself. After which, I don't know. I don't know whether I'll throw the box out or leave it there, because it was his box of green tea.

The tea tastes bitter and I don't like it. I know you're meant to drink it without sugar, the way he drank it. If everything were okay, I'd add sugar. No, I'd drink coffee, the way I've always done every morning. But now I have to finish his tea. It's bitter and tasteless. For me, right now, nothing should taste good. Hot and bitter suits me.

Around midday, my friend Maria drops by. I get up to open the door for her. When we go into the living room, she always sits in my chair. She never seems to wonder whether I might have been sitting there. She never notices the seat is warm, never asks herself, "Hang on a moment, was my friend sitting here, have I taken her chair?" That's Maria. She never wonders about anything. She arrived wearing a black miniskirt, sheer black tights, high-heeled boots, jacket, red blouse, red nails, lipstick, mascara, eyeliner, glitter eyeshadow, and loud earrings that twinkle and sway back and forth with every movement of her head. She's been to the hairdresser's. She's had a manicure. She smells of some godawful perfume, violent and bitter, which makes me want to throw up. But then again, I *should* feel like throwing up, and so I sit closer.

"I brought you some soup," says Maria.

"I'm not sick for you to have to bring me soup," I say. I know I'm being rude, but then again, my husband is dead.

"I made it for you today. If you don't eat, you'll get sick."

I don't say anything. She didn't need to get all dressed up just to come over. I light a cigarette.

"You should let some air in here," she tells me, as if it were her apartment. "It smells strange in here."

"You smell strange."

Maria sighs.

"Well, anyway, I've got to go. I'll drop by again tomorrow."

I stand by the window and watch as she walks toward the car in her high-heeled boots, her hips swaying from side to side, her coiffure bobbing up and down. With long, slender fingers tipped with painted nails, she rummages in her handbag looking for her car key. When she finds the key, she points it toward her gleaming, freshly-washed vehicle. The indicator lights come on and the car roars into life, as if it were pleased that Maria is about to hop inside and drive it away. A warm spring breeze ruffles her hair just as she climbs inside the car. The tender leaves and branches rustle, as if they were all saying: "Goodbye, Maria!" She drives away. She will laugh, flashing her perfect smile, she will giggle, make jokes, carry on with her life. The street is awash with crisp sunshine even after she has gone. Shortly thereafter, a girl and boy pass by. They're holding hands. They're laughing. The girl kisses the boy on the neck. Behind them walk two teenagers. They're talking loudly and laughing about something. They've all taken off their jackets. The sun makes them narrow their eyes, it highlights their freckles. How can they not be embarrassed? I can't help wondering. The world hasn't stopped, but Sveto—my world—is in the ground, where he's now decomposing. His body is cold, frozen, just as it was when I touched him as he lay in the coffin. The earth weighs down on him. They say the worms eat the dead. But how do they get in? Or are they engendered by the body itself? How is that possible? A car with blaring music stops in front of the building. The music is dreadful. I move away from the window.

I light a cigarette and stare at Maria's soup. Chicken soup, as if

I were sick. That's what I often made for Sveto. He really liked my chicken soup. I'd make him a huge pot, and he'd eat three bowls twice a day—for lunch and dinner. Sometimes he'd eat so much he'd get a stomachache. You make the best soup in the world, he'd say. Once, D asked me to bring him something to eat. Sveto was at work, so I put some of the soup in a jar and took it to D. Then we did what we did. When I got home, I saw he'd texted me to say the soup was delicious, but that next time I should bring him more because he's a man with a hearty appetite. A week later I made soup for Sveto again, but this time I made extra and gave D two jars. He texted that night: "Why so little? Next time, please make me a whole pot." He said that every week. And so once I made a huge pot of soup when Sveto was at work. I filled four jars, leaving only a little in the pot. When I got home that night, Sveto was waiting for me in the living room. "Honey, I'm a little cross with you," he said. "Why so little?"

My mom keeps calling me. I know she wants to come over and talk all kinds of nonsense. When she comes over she tries to lift my spirits, take my mind off what I'm going through. So she talks about her friends, about my brother's kids, and sometimes she brings up politics. It drives me up the wall. Still, I answer the phone and tell her she can come. Maybe one day she'll finally realize I don't want to see her, or anyone else for that matter.

She arrives in the evening. I recognize the sound she makes coming up the stairs. She stomps like a soldier. Her footsteps would wake a person in a coma. She goose-stepped at the funeral; even on solemn occasions she doesn't know how to conduct herself. She rings the doorbell repeatedly, short, sharp bursts to let me know it's her. I decide to linger on the couch, to leave her standing outside the door. That way, she might get the message that I don't want her coming around. She starts ringing again, which so annoys me that I get up and open the door.

"It smells of smoke in here," she says as she comes in, and begins opening the windows and balcony door.

"Leave them," I say, knowing she'll ignore me. Every time she comes over she acts like she owns the place, moving my things around, tidying up, opening doors and windows.

"Maybe you shouldn't smoke so much," she says, turning around, having opened up the whole place. The orange rays of the setting sun spread throughout the apartment. A scent of lindens wafts in. It rankles me to think that the world carries on even though Sveto is in the grave.

"Maybe you should mind your own business," I tell her, lighting up another cigarette.

Sitting down beside me she lets out a sigh.

She starts going on about her friend, Mira, about how Mira's boss mistreats her, about how when Mira's son got married, she didn't get any time off work to attend the wedding—or something like that. As ever, I don't listen to her. I focus on her mouth. She smoked for years and wrinkles formed around her lips from her constantly drawing on the cigarettes. They're especially noticeable on her upper lip whenever she rounds her mouth to articulate an "o" or a "u". Her orange lipstick, which looks dreadful on her and accentuates her sallow complexion, has bled into the wrinkles. When she widens her mouth to articulate an "e" or "a", I catch a glimpse of her tongue, marbled with a white film that makes her look sick. Her mouth should stink, but it doesn't. I can see she's lost an upper tooth. Her other teeth have yellowed, and those with crowns have darkened where the crown meets her receding gums, which also have a sickly look.

"Maybe you should see a dentist," I interject.

My mother stares down at her hands, which are folded in her lap. They're covered with liver spots.

"And you ought to get some decent lipstick. That one is bleeding into your wrinkles. Have you any idea what your mouth looks like?" I add. I know I'm being cruel, but I couldn't care less.

My mother sits gazing down at her prematurely aged hands. I notice she's wearing eyeliner and that it too has bled into her wrinkles. I want to tell her that, too.

"Where would I get the money to buy any, dear?" she says, looking up at me. Her eyes look teary. What right does she have to cry? I think to myself, and stare at her hands again. I notice there's a hole in her sleeve and her blouse is worn out. I say nothing and light another cigarette.

"Have you had anything to eat today, dear?" she says in a gentle voice. A voice she never used before Sveto was in the ground. I gesture with my hand to say I haven't.

"Would you like me to fix you something? Is there anything I can get you? You have to eat *something*, dear," she says, placing her hand on my knee. I bristle every time she touches me. I'm sick of feeling sorry about being cruel.

"Maria brought me some soup."

"Did you eat it?"

"No. You eat it. I don't want any."

My mother gets up and goes into the kitchen. From the living room, I can see her back. I see her lift the pot of soup that Maria brought me. Maria tied it with some stupid strap to make sure the lid wouldn't come off. My mother places it on the stove. Then she rests both hands on the counter and leans her head back, as if stretching her neck. I hear the faint sound of her whimpering. She lowers her head, and then slowly walks away. To the bathroom I imagine, where she remains for quite some time, while I sit on the couch smoking.

My mother returns to the kitchen and I hear the clatter of dishes and cutlery, of her putting something on the table, of her opening a cupboard door and then slamming it shut. She's never done anything gently. When I was a little girl and she dried my hair, she would always carelessly yank it and jab me with her fingernails.

"Come and keep me company," I hear her say as she sits down at the kitchen table. I feel like I have no choice. Once she's eaten, maybe she'll go home, and I won't have to throw out the soup.

On the table are two bowls of soup—I should have guessed.

"Didn't I tell you that I don't want anything to eat," I blurt, taking a deep drag on my cigarette.

"Who knows? You might feel hungry if you see me eating. You don't have to eat if you don't want to," she says. Steam rises from the bowl. As usual, the soup is scalding hot. She always overheats things. When I was a child, I burned my tongue a hundred times from eating her hot food. She'll heat up something for you as a favor and end up causing you pain.

"For once in your life, can't you learn not to cook things to death? Do you want me to burn my tongue?" I sit down in a huff. "Not that I'm going to eat, but if I *had* planned on eating, I wouldn't have wanted you to turn the soup into a scalding mush," I say, the words tumbling out of my mouth. My mother is silent. She strokes the spoon she's placed on her napkin. I again glance at her aging hands, her gnawed finger nails and the long furrows that have formed on them.

My mother sighs.

"Do you remember that time you were looking after your brother and you tried to heat up the leftover stew and burned yourself?" she asks me.

"Not really, but I know I have a scar from it." I hope the memory of it will pain her.

"Let me have a look at it," she says.

I hold out my left hand. At the base of my thumb is a pinkish mark in the shape of a rabbit. My mother tries to kiss it. I pull away from her in disgust.

"Your father was away at a seminar. He wasn't coming back till the next day. I was left all by myself with you and your brother. Your aunt or your grandmother, one or the other, was supposed to look after you, but at the last moment she couldn't come. And I had plans to meet a friend." She pauses, swallows. "He would have been very angry if I hadn't gone. I was in love with him." She looks straight into my eyes. "He'd mesmerized me. I'd leave work early so I could see him, or if there was some-one to look after you, I'd pretend I had to work an extra hour."

As my mother speaks, my mind goes blank.

"And that's why I asked you to look after your brother, because I was going to be back in a couple of hours. But a couple ended up being three. And your brother got hungry. And that's why you heated up the stew, because I told you if he was hungry, you should give him something to eat. But I never told you what to give him. And when I got home I could smell something burning, even from the ground floor. I ran up the stairs so fast I broke a heel. I could hear you screaming and your brother too. I rushed in and found the whole kitchen white with smoke.

The pot had spilled and there was burnt stew all over the floor. I could hear you howling in the bathroom. I walked in," she said, clutching the spoon, "and I saw you standing there holding your little hand under the running water, sobbing. Your brother—he seemed so small—was clinging to your leg. His face was all red and drenched with tears. He ran toward me when he saw me and grabbed my knees. I pushed him aside because then you turned around and I saw you, your mouth contorted, your eyes all swollen with tears, your face all flushed. Your brother hit his head on the washing machine and started wailing. You cried out when you saw me and started jumping up and down, saying over and over: 'It hurts, it hurts, it hurts.' And then I saw your poor little hand, all swollen from the burn. I wanted to die, my baby," my mother says, lowering her head, drawing her aged hand across her eyes.

My vision blurs as I notice something dripping into my soup. I lift the spoon to my mouth.

Adulterer

MY HUSBAND IS having an affair. Here's how I first found out: I always empty his pockets before putting his pants in the wash. There are usually a few coins, little wads of used chewing gum wrapped in tissue, and strands of loose tobacco. But this time there was also a crumpled receipt. I smoothed it out. *Marlboro, Orbit, Dureks.* Dureks? I wondered what Dureks might be. It cost 114 denars. Then, with horror, I realized that it must be "Durex." Condoms. There's no such thing as Durex gum, I said to myself. The same goes for Durex cigarettes or Durex bottled water. But first I wanted to make sure it was condoms if I was going to confront him with the receipt. I looked at the slip of paper again and saw the address. A Makpetrol gas station in Avtokomanda, about a twenty-minute drive from where we live, in the Vlae district of Skopje. I put the clothes in the washing machine, turned it on, climbed in my Citroën, and drove to the Makpetrol gas station in Avtokomanda.

I looked around to see whether they sold condoms. I was a little embarrassed, but the fear of what I might discover actually spurred me on. And then I spotted them: Durex condoms. I took a pack. I handed it to the cashier. I paid for it. She gave me a receipt. Printed on it was: "Dureks. 114 denars. Makpetrol Gas Station, Avtokomanda."

I drove home. The washing machine had finished its cycle. I hung my husband's and my children's clothes up to dry. I could have kicked myself for never having thought to smell his shirts or check them for lipstick stains, the way they do in the movies.

That's what I was thinking to myself as I hung out the laundry. I looked at my watch. It was seven o'clock. He said he'd be going to a business dinner after work, so I just heated up some leftovers for the kids. I sat in the living room and waited for him to come home. The receipt and the condoms were in the pocket of my sweater. At about ten o'clock, I heard his key turn in the lock, then his footsteps and the sound of him dropping his briefcase in the hallway as he hung his coat on the rack. My heart was pounding. I wondered what I would say or do if I found out he really was having an affair.

"Ta-a-a-nya," he called out from the hallway. "Come here!" he shouted angrily.

I ran to him straight away.

"What's with all this water here?" he pointed his finger at a small puddle on the floor near the coatrack.

"I don't know," I said, just as surprised as he was. "Maybe it's from Aneta's umbrella." And Sasho's umbrella, I thought to myself.

"Well, mop it up," he said, and he went into the living room. He sat down on the couch, picked up the remote, and started flipping through channels as I mopped up the water.

He'd ruined my moment. I had imagined myself saying, "Sit down, Zoran. We need to have a little talk." Then, as I sat opposite him I would have boldly slid the receipt across the table, pointed at the word "Dureks," and said, "What's this?" I didn't know what would have happened after that.

After I'd mopped up the water in the hallway, I went back to the living room and sat down in the armchair opposite him.

"Zoran," I said. He didn't turn around. "Zoran," I repeated.

"Mm?" he said, without taking his eyes off the TV, tilting his chin upward slightly.

"I found this in your pocket." I took out the receipt. My hands were shaking, so I threw it on the table and clasped my hands in my lap.

"Yeah, what is it?" he said, glancing at it briefly, then carried on watching TV.

"A receipt," I said, trying to keep my voice steady. "Why did you buy condoms?" I demanded, feeling braver.

I'd finally gotten his attention.

"Condoms? What are you talking about?" he rose from the couch a little way and snatched the receipt off the table. He held it up at arm's length, because he needs reading glasses to see things up close.

"You bought cigarettes, gum and Durex from the gas station in Avtokomanda. What were you doing over there? Why did you buy condoms?"

"What is it with you? Have you suddenly lost your mind?" he said, and threw the receipt down on the table. He stared at me with contempt. I didn't know what to say. I clamped my lips together so I wouldn't burst into tears.

"How the fuck should I know where I got this receipt. Anyway, how do you know it's mine?"

"It was in your pocket!"

"So what! Maybe I picked it up by accident in the shop."

There was some logic to that, I suppose. But then I remembered the cigarettes and the gum.

"But didn't you buy cigarettes and gum?"

"You stupid idiot! Am I the only one who smokes that brand of cigarettes or chews gum? Don't give me this crap," he said, settling back down on the couch with the remote in his hands. He was still scowling.

I didn't know what to say, so I said nothing.

"You and your crazy shit again," he muttered angrily. "You imagine things, you snoop around, and you poke your nose where it doesn't belong."

"That's not true," I said.

"Oh, bullshit," he snapped back. "You need your head examined. Going through my pockets."

"That's not true. I was checking your pants pockets before putting them in the mach—" He didn't let me finish.

"Oh, bullshit! Don't you go through my phone as well? And read my emails?"

"That only happened once!" I lied, defensively, my eyes filling with tears.

"Oh quit blubbering. You're sick. You're always imagining

things," he said and stomped off to take a shower. Half an hour later, he shouted for me to bring him his underpants, a T-shirt, and his bathrobe.

After that, I started going through his phone more often, although it was a bit harder than before. He nearly always kept his phone in his pocket and rarely left it lying around the apartment. Whenever he did, I would have to go through it quickly to check if he'd gotten any messages. But because I wasn't familiar with that make of phone, I couldn't go through it fast enough to be sure that the screen would turn off before I put it back where he'd left it. In addition, I was no longer able to access to his emails after he changed his password. I tried to guess what it might be: the last time it had been his name and year of birth. That was simple. I now tried our kids' names and their dates of birth, but no luck. I even tried my own name, in various combinations—Tanya, Tanny, Tatjana—but no luck. Even though I knew that if he chose a name as his password it would be one of the kids' names, I was still disappointed. My attempts to guess his password somehow resulted in his e-mail getting blocked. He said nothing to me about it, which made me even more suspicious. Maybe he thought it was some other woman doing the same thing—going through his email—and he was hiding that from me too? I had started doing this long before I found out about the new woman. I was never aware of any others before that, even though I regularly read his e-mails and went through his phone. But still, I always had my suspicions.

The second sure sign came a few weeks later, when he came home from work very late. He'd warned me—he said that he'd be going out to dinner, that he'd be working late because he had to close a business deal with some people from Switzerland. He said he would have to drive them all over city, if required, and he didn't know what time he'd be home. He got back around two in the morning. Obviously, I wasn't asleep, but I pretended I was. I heard him come in, take off his shoes, take off his jacket, enter the bathroom. The faucet ran for much longer than usual. He was cleaning himself up. He normally doesn't take that long to get washed before bed. Then he went to the living room and turned on the TV. He fell asleep there. I went in and kissed him as he slept. "What the hell? Why did you wake me up?" he growled. He was probably surprised that I'd kissed him. I wanted only to smell him, not to kiss him. He smelled of soap. And of perfume. The third sign that something was definitely going on did indeed have something to do with his phone. Here's how it came about: One day Zoran went to bed after he came home from work. He told me to wake him at eight-fifteen because he had to go out to dinner with some business partners. He said the dinner reservation was for nine, which seemed unusually late. But my mom called, inviting me over for coffee—something she rarely does. I asked my daughter to wake him instead. To be honest, I didn't want to wake him at all, because I had a feeling that he wouldn't be going to where he said he was going. But I didn't want to admit it at the time. Anyway, when I got home from my mom's he was still asleep, even though it was almost ten. My daughter wasn't at home. Then I saw she'd sent me a message telling me she'd be going out and for me to call Dad and wake him. I went into the bedroom and woke him. He got up, groggy and moody, the way he always is just after waking up. "What time is it!" he said sleepily. "Why didn't you wake me up!" he shouted when he saw that he was forty-five minutes late. At first, I tried explaining but then I realized something very important: Not one of his business partners had called to ask where he was. "Why didn't your friends call if you're so late?" I asked, staring at him defiantly. For the first time in my life, I saw him look confused. He didn't even open his mouth. He just shot out of the room and went into the bathroom, where he let the water run for a long time. I sat there on our bed, hanging my head, staring blankly at my feet. His phone was on the bedside table. I didn't notice it until a message came through. I looked at the screen: no name, just a number. The text was simply: "???" Then the screen went black. But I memorized the number and quickly wrote it down on a scrap of paper.

I decided to confide in my friend and neighbor, Sandra. Every day at around six in the evening, Sandra and I would get together for coffee. If my husband was at home, we'd go to her place instead. She's a widow. The next day, I told her everything. Sandra offered to call the number I'd written down. We had to find out whether it was a male or a female voice. Even get a name if we could. But that was impossible—how do you get the person you're calling to introduce themselves? However, Sandra was amazing. She didn't hesitate or need time to prepare—she just grabbed her cell phone and made the call.

"Hello, good evening," she said confidently, politely. "I have a missed call from this number. To whom am I speaking?" There was silence on the other end. "My name is Sandra Stojanovska," she said, giving a fake surname. "And you are?" she asked in a polite, friendly tone. Another short pause. "I'm sorry, there must be some mistake. I really have no idea what happened. In any event, I'm sorry to have disturbed you," she said and hung up.

"Her name's Emilia," said Sandra, looking at me with concern. "Do you know her?"

It took me some time to realize what Sandra was asking me. She shook my elbow. "Are you okay?" she said. She brought me a glass of water and ordered me to drink it. My insides were churning but I also felt a kind of emptiness. That's what happens when your insides get all messed up, I thought to myself.

"There's an Emilia who works with him," I told my friend. I felt even worse as I remembered everything my husband once happened to tell me. "A young assistant. In other words, much younger than me." I kept taking sips of water because my mouth was getting so dry. "He told me they have a lot of ambitious young people working on the team. And that they were new. Hired a little less than a year ago." I tried to recall what she looked like, but I'd never seen a photo of her. I imagined her as petite and slender, with a small, thin nose, blue eyes, and glossy hair with highlights.

I was throwing up constantly for the next two days. Everyone at home thought I was sick. I stayed in bed all day but got up to fix lunch and dinner, as usual, and in the morning to lay out Zoran's clothes, to find socks that matched his suit, to knot his tie, to make his coffee and see him off. While he was shaving in the bathroom, I was vomiting there next to him, in the toilet bowl. Secretly, I wanted him to see me throwing up, to know that I was sick because of him. But he didn't see a thing, he just carried on looking at himself in the mirror and shaving. He's quite moody in the morning before work. And when he comes home at night he's exhausted. That night and the next night he came home very late. He didn't answer when I called him, or else he picked up and told me he was in a meeting. The first night he came home smelling of perfume. I don't know if it was because of that scent, but I went into the bathroom and threw up again. When I went back to bed he was asleep, so he didn't even notice anything was wrong with me.

Sandra said it would take her a couple of days to find out about Emilia and if there was anything going on between her and Zoran. She told me she knew some people who worked at the company. She could get them to sniff around, do a bit of investigating. I went over to her place, supposedly just for our usual coffee and chat, even though I felt like I had rocks in my stomach.

Sandra gave me an anxious look. She told me to sit down. She took my hand and peered into my eyes. Then she told me everything. There were rumors going around about them. They stayed at the office till late to work on projects. She'd got a promotion probably because of him. "Yet," Sandra added, "they say she's quite competent at her job. She's twenty-seven." In other words, I thought to myself, she's fourteen years younger than me, seventeen years younger than him. But just wait until she starts getting stretch marks, cellulite, fat thighs, and flab around her middle. The little slut hasn't given birth yet, I thought to myself.

Sandra took my hand. "Everything in the universe consists of energy. Whatever energy you release comes back to you, so you have to think about everything positively. Absorb positive energy from the universe, liberate yourself from negative energy, and you'll find balance. Breathe in through your nose," Sandra commanded, shutting her eyes. She lifted her chin high and breathed deeply, tickling the air with her fingertips each time she inhaled. I breathed through my nose. Once, twice, three times. "Your thoughts will be cleansed now," said Sandra, as her hot hand pressed mine. "I'm giving you energy," she said. "Do you feel it?"

I nodded. Then I said, "Give me your phone. I want to call her and hear her voice."

After that, I called her three days in a row. I'd call, then hang up. I found a way to hide my number. She'd pick up, I'd hang up. I found out her home phone number too. I'd call her at home and a thin, shaky voice would answer. "Hello, can I speak to Emilia?" "Who's calling?" And I'd hang up.

"Her mother's got MS. They live alone. Her father remarried. And just imagine, instead of staying at home to take care of her mother, she goes out to work," said Sandra, with a look of contempt. I mirrored her look. What else can I say about that little slut, that Emilia, other than she doesn't look after her mom, and in high school she was with a guy for three years, and when she broke it off he got depressed and even contemplated suicide. That was the only compromising information I could dig up. Oh and, of course, the fact that she was fucking a married man, a father of two, who was seventeen years older than she.

That's exactly what I told Emilia's mother when I called her. That day Zoran came home early from work. He looked gray, and he was very angry.

"You've put carrots in the soup again!" he shouted from the kitchen after he sat down to eat. "You know I hate carrots!" he yelled.

"Sorry. I didn't think you'd be eating at home," I said in a voice that told him I knew he wasn't yelling at me because of the carrots.

"You're useless! What else do you have to do besides cook? Huh? Can't you do anything right?" he growled.

I burst into tears.

"What's wrong with you? Why are you blubbering?" he said, a bit calmer now, but still gray in the face.

"You're having an affair," I could barely get the words out.

His face went even grayer.

"I beg your pardon?" That's what he always says when he's annoyed with me. He makes me repeat what I was afraid to say.

"You're having an aff—" I didn't finish the word because I suddenly hiccupped, which made me cry even harder.

I didn't have the strength to look him in the face. I knew that he turns gray and then red when he's furious. I also knew he knew I was the one who'd called. And that he knew I knew. Because now I *knew* I was right all along. About the other times—maybe I really had been seeing things that weren't there, as he'd claimed, because for years there was no proof of anything. He would always come home after work and play with the kids. We used to make love, too.

"I'm not going to bother defending myself against false accusations. You're imagining things again," he said, twirling his finger at his temple as if to suggest I was cuckoo.

A wave of panic came over me. I thought that if I didn't keep on crying and shouting I might fall apart. I didn't give a damn about anything—whether he shouted at me, whether the kids heard us from the other room, or even whether he shoved me or hit me.

"E—mi—li—a," I sobbed, barely getting the words out. "Your assistant. I know. I know!" I shouted. I shouted "I know" over and over.

I don't remember much of what happened next—he smashed a plate; I cleaned up the kitchen. He went out; I locked myself in the bedroom, took a couple of Diazepam and fell asleep. The kids were in their bedrooms. But they're not that young anymore. They can fix their own dinner.

We didn't speak for the next few days. He rarely answered his phone, or when he did, he would snap at me: I'm at work, I'm in a meeting, I'm at dinner. He came home at dawn to sleep. He slept on the couch in the living room. He didn't eat. When he came home, he smelled of kebabs, rakija, perfume—that slut Emilia's perfume. Her cell phone was switched off. So was her landline.

Sandra read my coffee grounds.

"You have a heavy burden from which a big plan is brewing. But the plan, which is like a huge wave, is encountering an obstacle in its path. Like the wave that smashes everything in its path, you need to smash through that obstacle in order to achieve your goal. Relief and remorse await on the other side. Someone's going to be sorry—I see a figure crying. Do you see it?" she said, showing me the cup. All I saw was brown sludge—thicker on one side of the cup—and a few scattered spots.

"Sandra, I have to follow Zoran at least once to see where he goes, to see where that slut who wants to ruin my life lives," I suddenly heard myself say. "Please, can we use your car? I'll hide in the back. You drive. Do you have a wig?"

Sandra agreed to go along with my plan. The next day we went out and bought some wigs. She got herself a long blond one, while I opted for a short black one with bangs. We pulled into the parking lot at his office building. We got there at five, which is when he finishes work. His Mercedes was there. We parked near it. I sat in the back of Sandra's Fiat, so I could hide when he came out of the building. We waited. We smoked a few cigarettes. We did some breathing exercises. Sandra talked to me about the importance of having balanced energy and how she achieved it. She described her meditation exercises, told me about her life coach and the types of books she read. She recommended a few books about how to balance your energy and told me that they would help me with my current "difficult journey," as she called it. At times I felt awkward about dragging Sandra into the whole mess but then I quickly brushed such thoughts from my mind. I had enough troubles without having to worry about Sandra. My stomach kept churning and gurgling, like it had when I found that receipt in Zoran's pocket. After two hours of waiting in Sandra's car, Zoran finally appeared. He was in no hurry and he seemed to be smiling. I crouched down on the floor behind the front seat of the Fiat and peeked out at him. He got into his Mercedes. He turned the key in the ignition, but didn't drive off. He was waiting. Then she appeared. She ran out of the building, looking down at the ground. She was nothing like I'd imagined. "She looks like you," Sandra whispered. Only younger, I thought. Something was going on in my throat, in my head; my throat clenched, my head spun. And suddenly things became clear. "Follow them," I said to Sandra when they took off.

We followed them all the way to Avtokomanda. They parked in a small lot in front of an old Soviet-style building. Sandra and I parked a bit farther down the street, and waited. We waited seventeen minutes. We couldn't see what was going on inside the car, because Zoran had had the windows tinted about a year ago. I no longer needed to wonder why he'd done that. I wanted to go over and tap on the window. I told Sandra what I felt like doing. She warned me that it was too soon to take such a drastic step. It seemed to me that maybe she didn't want to get too mixed up in the whole business. Anyway, I don't think I should have listened to her; I should have gone over and caught them right in the act. Seventeen minutes later, the little slut got out of the car and walked into an apartment building. Building 2A. I didn't know which floor or which apartment, but I knew I could easily find out.

We continued following him. He stopped in Debar Maalo. Sandra got out after him and came back fifteen minutes later. She told me that he'd sat down in one of the cafés—alone—and ordered something to eat.

"I saw you," I said to him when he came home and lay down on the couch in front of the TV.

He looked at me, confused, puzzled. A sense of courage, mixed with panic, rose within me.

"I know what's going on. I saw you both. When you drove her home. In Avtokomanda."

This time all the blood drained from his face; he was neither gray nor red.

"This has got to stop. I don't intend to let a common little *slut* destroy my marriage," I said, raising my voice.

"What has gotten into you?" His face turned red again. His double chin trembled.

"If you don't stop seeing her, I'll call the CEO and tell him everything. Both of you will lose your jobs," I threatened, because I didn't want to tell him to leave. He couldn't leave me alone with the kids.

"You're CRAZY," he shouted. He slammed his fist down on the glass coffee table and it shattered. I got scared and my courage dissipated. "You FOLLOWED me!" he yelled. "When I was taking a work colleague *home*. Which is a *normal* thing to do. For God's sake, she's my assistant. We work together!"

He was standing up, leaning over me, yelling in my face. "You *live* off my earnings. You go to a *manicurist*, a *pedicurist*, a *beautician* with the money I bring home. You drive an *expensive* car. You buy *expensive clothes*. And now you're poking your nose in my affairs? You cow, you piece of trash, fuck you!" he yelled. Then he grabbed his coat, quickly put his shoes on, and left. We didn't speak for several days after that. He started coming home late from work, or coming home and then going out again at night, so I thought up a new plan. I found an old Dictaphone around the house, on which my daughter had recorded make-believe radio shows when she was little. I waited for a day when he'd get home from work early, because I knew that then he'd be going out again the same night. I went outside and put the Dictaphone in the Mercedes, under the front passenger seat. I switched it on. The next day, I got up to lay his clothes out for work and made his breakfast, and while he was taking his shower, I went to retrieve the Dictaphone. It was still there. When he left for work, I turned it on and listened.

First there was a long silence, then the sound of someone getting into the car, and the car starting. Him coughing, singing, swearing at other drivers. A loud fart. Driving. Talking on the phone. "Hey, I'm on my way. I'll be out in front of your building in ten minutes. I'll honk. See you soon." Engine noises. Speeding up, slowing down. The radio being turned on. Music. Music and ads for five or six minutes. After that, the radio being switched off. The door opening. "What took you so long, gorgeous? You're late again." Then a thin female voice, the same one that said hello when I called the cell phone number I'd memorized: "What? Only two minutes? Grumpy!" Laughter. Then just silence and music. The engine starting up. The female voice: "I love this song!" and the music being turned up. Then the Dictaphone stopped because it had run out of memory.

That evening when he got back from work, he lay down on the couch again. I sat down in the armchair.

"I want to have a talk with you," I said, hiding the Dictaphone behind my back.

"We have nothing to say to each other until you start acting normal again. And as far as I can see, that hasn't happened yet."

"I want you to admit that you have a mistress and to stop seeing her."

"I don't have any mistress to stop seeing. I want you to admit that you're crazy and to stop all this nonsense."

"You won't admit it?" I said, as that strange courage once again swelled inside me, making my hands sweat and shake. The Dictaphone, with my finger on the play/pause button, almost slipped out of my hand.

"I have nothing to admit," he spat. His eyes were bloodshot.

I took out the Dictaphone. "What took you so long, gorgeous? You're late again.'" A thin female voice: "What? Only two minutes? Grumpy!" Laughter. I stopped it at that moment, like in the movies.

Zoran got up and tried to grab the Dictaphone. I gripped it tightly with both hands. He grabbed my arm, he squeezed my fingers. My eyes watered in pain. He snatched the Dictaphone and threw it out the window. He was breathing hard through his nose. I'd never seen him so furious.

"Go to your mother's. I can't stand the sight of you. You make me *sick*," he said.

"*I* make *you* sick?" I tried to say, but the words came out in puffs. I was panting like a dog and I couldn't stop.

"They're my kids. I'm not going anywhere without them," I somehow managed to say. "You go to your mother's," I said, and then went to throw up.

"This is my apartment! Do you fucking hear me, you crazy bitch!" he screamed and slammed the front door. He left.

That afternoon, I did in fact go to my mom's. We sat in the kitchen, at the table where she always drinks coffee with her friends when they come over. I burst into tears.

"Pull yourself together," she said to me. I tried to do as I was told. Her red lipstick was slightly smudged on the right side of her mouth and her mascara had run a bit below her left eye, clumping in the wrinkles under her eyelashes. She was holding a nail polish brush in her long bony fingers. She started painting her nails as I told her what had happened.

"He's your husband. You chose him, so you have to put up with him. Divorce is out of the question," she said, blowing on the red polish that coated her long pointy nails. "You can't kick him out, because he may never come back," she said, looking me in the eye. "Listen to me, darling. I'm talking from experience. *She's* the one who needs to go."

So I hatched my final plan. I took me a few days to arrange it. I bought a short shovel and a bottle of water, and when I knew for certain that he'd be going out that night, I got dressed up as if I were going out too. I put on makeup and some killer heels, dabbed on a bit of perfume, took his spare car keys, and of course my cell phone, which I switched to silent mode. I went downstairs, opened the trunk of his Mercedes, and curled up inside. I slammed it shut and waited. Outside I heard footsteps, voices, people laughing or talking on the phone. A thin beam of light from the streetlamp was shining through a chink in the trunk. An hour went by. Then Zoran got in the car. Before he started the engine, he rummaged around, probably searching for another hidden Dictaphone. He turned the music on loud and drove off. He drove for twenty minutes, presumably to Avtokomanda. He stopped. Someone got in the car. I could hear a female voice. Laughter. Then a lively conversation over the music as the car drove on and on. Then it started to climb a hill, took a few bends, tossing me left and right. There was no longer any light seeping through the chink in the trunk. My ears started to pop. I realized he was driving up Mount Vodno. The car stopped, but the music continued. Then there was some jazz, something smoother, but still loud. Their voices went quiet. Occasionally I could hear a word or two, brief laughter or an exclamation. Then the car started rocking. I started to tap the shovel on the floor of the trunk in sync with the rocking. Lightly at first, then louder and louder. The rocking stopped. The music was turned off. *What is that? What is that?* they both said. I could hear the faint sounds of clothes being pulled on. *What the hell is that?* Zoran's voice said again. I kept tapping with the shovel handle. I could hear footsteps outside the car. The door of the trunk clicked open. I saw them standing in front of me, looking all disheveled. I leapt out, brandishing the shovel above my head.

Genes

EVERY TIME NENAD did something bad, Gene would blame someone in my family, usually my grandfather. "It's in the genes," he'd say. "There's no escaping your genes." He singled out my grandfather because my grandfather was a gambler and a thief who'd spent time in jail. When he got out of prison my grandmother somehow managed to kick him out. But one day he came back, drunk, and assaulted her. She was bathing her four-year-old daughter, my mother, when he burst into the bathroom, grabbed my grandmother and beat her up, breaking her nose. Her nose remained crooked for the rest of her life. When her brothers heard what happened, they beat up my grandfather so badly that he never came back. A few months later, he was burnt to death in his apartment. He probably owed someone money.

The first time Gene mentioned my grandfather was after Nenad stole a bar of chocolate from a store. Nenad was just four years old at the time. I caught him stuffing chocolate in his mouth in the bathroom, hiding behind the shower curtain. Despite all the mischief he got up to, and despite the distrustful look in his eyes and the cynical twist to his mouth, right then he still looked somehow sweet, standing there in the tub with his shoes on and his face covered in chocolate. "Gene, Gene, Gene!" I shouted to my husband. And though Nenad was a brave child and always tried to hide his fear—as he did all his other feelings—his eyes widened and he became startled when I started shouting. Gene rushed into the bathroom and caught him red-handed with the half-eaten chocolate in his hand. "He stole it," I said, ratting on the child. "Just now, when we were at the store. He asked me to buy it for him and I said no, but he went ahead and took it anyway, without paying." Gene—or Eugene, to give his full name—thought of himself as somewhat high-minded and noble. He claimed never to have lied or stolen anything in his life and prided himself on always being compassionate to others. "Nomen est omen," he'd often say—though quite what he meant by that was never clear. Now his face darkened with anger and he grabbed Nenad by his T-shirt and yanked him out of the shower. The chocolate bar flew out of Nenad's sticky hands and landed, grossly, in the tub. Gripping the boy with one hand, Gene started smacking his buttocks and the backs of his legs. "No . . . son . . . of . . . mine . . . is . . . going . . . to . . . be . . . a . . . thief!" he yelled, each word accompanied with a hard smack. Nenad squirmed and tried to wriggle free, but Gene held onto him so firmly he couldn't escape. "Don't you ever do anything like this again! Do you understand?" he yelled. But Nenad just opened his mouth in the shape of an O and started to bawl. "So you want some more, do you?" Gene asked, acting the tough guy, though I could tell it wasn't easy for him to beat the boy. "No-o-o," Nenad wailed, louder and louder until eventually I just pulled him out of the bathroom, terrified of what the neighbors might think if they heard. God forbid they ever find out he's been stealing, I thought to myself. They'd never let him back in the building.

Nenad lay down on his bed and turned his face to the wall, whimpering quietly now. He didn't react when I touched him. I sat on the side of the bed and gave him a lecture on stealing. I told him that if he stole things, he'd wind up in jail. But since he didn't react to either my caresses or my words I left him there and went to the living room. Gene was sitting staring at a blank TV screen.

"Maybe you shouldn't have beaten him so hard," I said. "He's really upset."

"Well? And aren't *you* upset that your son's a little thief? Weren't you the one who called me to deal with the situation? Why did you yell out 'Gene, Ge-e-ene' if you're going to question my actions?" he asked, screwing up his mouth as he imitated my voice. "Why don't *you* do something, huh?"

"Maybe I should have just bought him the chocolate," I said. "Stealing is totally unacceptable under any circumstances!" Gene blustered. "It's irrelevant whether or not we buy him anything. It's something that has to be made crystal clear to him, and that's why he was taught this lesson." Gene lit a cigarette, as he did whenever he was worked up. And that was when he brought up the subject of my grandfather. He didn't mention him by name, but I knew he was thinking of him.

"It's not as if the boy doesn't know the difference between right and wrong. We've always taught him the right values. He's been well brought up and showered with attention. Not like other kids. But sometimes, you know, it just hasn't got anything to do with the parents. This criminal behavior has no connection with how he's been brought up. It's in his genes. Traits passed down from generation to generation. The family traits," he said, looking at me meaningfully.

It wasn't the first time he'd brought up the subject of genes. He had a "theory" that every ethnic group had certain genetic traits that made them behave in particular ways. He even entertained certain strong convictions about what the men and women of different nationalities were like. Polish women were "greedy," for example, while American women were "proud." Macedonian women made the best wives, Montenegrins made the worst. But the vilest things he had to say were about the Greeks and the Albanians, or "Shiptars" as he insultingly referred to the latter. He despised the Greeks wholeheartedly, though he had little specific to say about them other than that the men were short and dark skinned, while the women had "big butts." More generally, he referred to the Greeks as "history's thieves." Sometimes when he got drunk with his friends he'd start talking about ancient Macedonia, pounding his fists on the table. These rants didn't interest me in the slightest. The past doesn't mean much to me. Nor did his tirades interest his friends, I realized, since they were obviously starting to avoid him. "Why do you think I know so many languages?" he'd ask them. "Why do you think it is that I can speak almost every language in Europe?" (And it was genuinely the case that he had taught himself to speak quite a few European languages.) "Yeah, yeah, we all know why," his friends would tease. "It's because you're so smart!" Then Gene would shake his head and wag his finger at them. "Wrong!" he'd bellow. "It's because Macedonian is the root of all languages!" However, he saved the worst insults for the Albanians. "Primitive and bloodthirsty! Stubborn and pig-headed!" he'd say. "I'm not talking about all of them, of course. One of my best friends is a Shiptar . . . They're not all alike. But they all stick together in the end. And one day, mark my words! they'll gobble us Macedonians up." On this last point he was especially insistent.

Nenad did not learn his "lesson" and continued to steal. Small things mostly, and only from time to time, but often enough to prompt Gene to start making direct references to my grand-father. We'd find things hidden under the boy's bed or stuffed into the folds of his clothes in his wardrobe. Little plastic figu-rines, colored pencils, chocolate bars, chewing gum, stickers and trading cards. Sometimes I wouldn't say a word to Gene about it. I'd leave the stolen items where I found them and pretend not to have seen anything. Once, however, I came across a larger and more expensive-looking toy: a shiny new model car that wasn't familiar to me. Nenad was doing a jigsaw puzzle when I asked him whom the car belonged to. "It's mine," he said. And when I asked him where he'd got it from, he told me, "Dad bought it for me." "When?" "The day before yesterday," he answered, not lifting his gaze from the puzzle. It all seemed suspicious to me. Gene was watching TV in the living room when I showed him the car and asked him whether he'd bought it for Nenad. His face darkened with anger as if he were already convinced the boy had stolen it. He told me to bring Nenad into the living room for a "talk."

"Where did you get this?" Gene demanded, waving the toy in front of Nenad's face.

Nenad was silent.

Gene shook him by the shoulder. "Where did you get it?"

Nenad's face screwed up and his eyes filled with tears. But I could see it was only a defense mechanism. This was always how he manipulated us. I felt so angry with him that I whacked the back of his head and told him to answer when his father asked him a question. He stumbled forward from the blow and burst into a fit of sobbing.

"Answer the question!" Gene commanded, towering over him like a sergeant major.

"I found it!" Nenad wailed. "I found it!" he kept on repeating, no matter how many times we insisted he admit what he'd done. But he refused to confess. We found out whom he'd stolen it from only when the mother of his friend next door phoned to suggest, politely, that Nenad might have "accidentally borrowed" Stevo's new toy car the last time he was at their place.

"There's no such toy here," Gene said. "You've made a mistake."

But the mother persisted until Gene grew indignant and started shouting. He told her that there were no thieves in our family and that we raised our little boy with love and care. Such a crime could simply never happen in our family, he said, but if the toy was so important to her then he'd give her the money to buy a new one. "Give me your bank account details!" he shouted, infuriated, repeating his absurd command until Stevo's mother finally hung up.

As soon as the call was over, Gene locked Nenad in the closet for two hours. "Do you want to see what happens to thieves?" he yelled as he shoved him into the dark. "They go to jail! Do you want to find out what jail is like? Good!" Then he turned the key.

At first, we waited and listened to Nenad crying, but after about ten minutes he stopped and we went and sat down in the living room. Gene lit a cigarette. (I'd stopped smoking at the time, since I was pregnant.) We were both trying to convince ourselves we'd done the right thing by locking the child in the closet.

"We have to be stricter with him," I said. "It won't do him any real harm; it'll just scare him a little." I was trying to reassure myself, hoping that Gene would try to make me feel better about things too.

"Children need to be trained, just like puppies," declared Gene confidently. "Who knows what kinds of problems we'll have later on if he doesn't learn now. We have to apply the principle of reward and punishment." Far from reassuring me that everything would turn out all right, however, Gene's absolute sense of certainty disturbed me. I wanted to see some sign that locking Nenad in the closet was difficult for him too. But Gene was a master at hiding his feelings. I nodded along in agreement with him, though secretly I was angry. From time to time, Gene turned his head in the direction of the closet, but not another sound came from therein.

"It appears the 'bad' genes are more potent in him than the good," said Gene, giving me a meaningful look. "The genes from his grandfather, that is, which is why it's so vital we act now to suppress his negative instincts. Because if we don't stamp them out, well, then . . ." And Gene made a gesture with his hand as if to suggest everything would go to hell.

"Why do you keep harping on about my grandfather? What's he got to do with any of this?" I snapped, angry enough now to pick a fight.

"What's your grandfather got to do with all this, you ask? What *hasn't* he got to do with it? A gambler and a thief. A kleptomaniac. And we know how he ended up. Do you really think such abnormalities aren't passed down the generations? Where else would the boy have gotten his instinct to steal?"

"Maybe it's us. Maybe we've done something wrong," I said, voicing what I feared most.

"Like what?" he asked. "Do you mean by bringing him up with parents who love and care for him? By giving him his own room in a beautiful apartment in the center of the city? By showering him with toys and lavishing him with love and attention?"

"I don't know," I said. "Maybe it's a different type of attention he's looking for?"

"Well he's getting a different type attention right now. He's finding out what punishment means. And when he's done, I'll tell him about your grandfather too, so he knows exactly how he'll end up if he carries on like this."

True to his word, after we let Nenad out of the closet, Gene sat the boy down in the living room and told him the story of my grandfather.

Nenad sat there on the couch about a yard away from his father, red and puffy-eyed, occasionally letting out a hiccup or sniffle, but trying his best to pretend he hadn't been crying. His hands were folded in his lap and he stared down at his feet, the tips of his toes pointing toward each other, dangling just short of the floor. And yet there was something no longer childlike about him. In his red eyes there was anger laced with resentment and a desire for revenge—the same look I saw in Gene's eyes when he was angry. His mouth hung open slightly, giving the impression that he doubted the words his father was telling him. Occasionally he'd lift his eyes to the ceiling, as if everything he was hearing were boring and pointless. When Gene noticed that Nenad wasn't really listening, he started to tell the story very differently and in much more graphic detail—the way you'd usually tell it to an adult. When he finally got to the part where my grandfather was burnt alive, Nenad let out a hiccup, shuddered slightly, opened his eyes wide, and shut his mouth. "Do you get it now? Do you understand what happens to liars and thieves?" Gene asked. "Yes," said Nenad, in a voice I barely recognized. "Good. Now come and give Daddy a hug and let's make up," said Gene, pulling the boy to him and hugging him tightly. But Nenad didn't hug him back. There was that same cynical look in his eyes, and his body was as limp as a ragdoll in Gene's grip.

After he'd been locked in the closet, Nenad became even stranger—more secretive and withdrawn. Even as a baby he'd seemed strange. There was something unnerving in his look, and sometimes, instead of love or warmth, I saw only emptiness in his eyes—a slight malice even. Then there were times when he'd become oddly absent and sit motionless in front of his toys for minutes at a time. Other times he'd have fits of stubborn rage and refuse to eat for days. "He's just like my mother," Gene would say proudly. "Resilient and headstrong, determined to get his own way." Back then he still used to try to spin our little boy's negative traits as qualities we could be proud of. Gene's own mother was a widow who'd raised two children on her own: himself and his sister Vaska. Neither my mother-in-law nor Vaska could exactly be described as shining embodiments of virtue. Both were replete with bad traits that might well have been passed down through their genes. But as Gene was very sensitive when it came to family matters, I kept this observation to myself for now, saving it for a more opportune moment, like an ace up my sleeve. Gene also used to claim that Nenad took after his side of the family physically, too. "He's got big green eyes just like my father," he'd say, knowing full well that Nenad looked nothing like his father and a lot more like me. Partly it was because Gene was always keen to find nice things to say about his father, a man he idealized because he'd died so young, in a train crash. If it wasn't some alleged resemblance to his father then it was some other small way in which Nenad physically resembled Gene's side of the family: his chin, his forehead, even his posture. But when our second son was born, Gene stopped trying to prove Nenad was "his," focusing his attention on the baby instead, and on all the many ways he took after Gene's side of the family.

We named our new baby Bozhidar, "God's gift." It is painful and shameful for me to admit but during my pregnancy, especially at night, when Gene and Nenad were asleep, there were times when I prayed the child wouldn't be like Nenad. A child who wouldn't lie and steal. A child I could understand. Gentle and naive, as innocent as a lamb, as good as gold: Bozhidar. When I had such thoughts, often I'd get up and kiss Nenad's little fingers as he lay asleep—his thieving little fingers, long and slender as scallion stalks.

All through my pregnancy, Nenad had acted as if nothing was happening. We told him how he'd soon have a little brother or sister and he'd just say, "Okay." "Which would you like the most, a brother or a sister?" we'd ask him. "It's all the same to me," he'd reply in his new "adult" tone, which was more disconcerting than amusing. When Bozho was born—the miracle I'd prayed for, Mummy and Daddy's precious little lamb—Nenad asked us how long the baby would be living with us. "Ha, ha, ha," we both laughed aloud, though neither of us found it funny, since he said it with that conniving look of his, the look that Gene and I never talked about. "He's your little brother," said Gene, "you have to look after him. The same way I have a sister and

your mother has a brother she loves. Now you have *Bo-zho-o-o!*"
And he began cooing at the baby, tickling its nose and chin, as
small as buttons.

Gene's words got me wondering how much I really did love
my own brother. When Mom got sick, before we'd even told her
the doctor's prognosis that her cancer was terminal, I went to the
bank and withdrew all the money from her account. And then
when she was admitted to hospital I took all of her jewelry out
of the safe and pawned it. Later, when my brother asked me for
a loan because he and his wife had both lost their jobs, I lied to
him that I didn't have any money to lend. Two months later we
bought a new car we didn't even need. Further back, when my
brother was only a baby, I remembered how I'd only pretended
to love him so that our parents would leave me alone with him.
Once, I picked him up and made him sit by the hot stove until
he started to scream from the heat searing his back. Many times
as we were growing up he would show me the scar to remind
me how wicked I was.

Nenad didn't even pretend to show affection toward Bozho.
He behaved toward him as if he were an object. Bozho was a calm
baby and hardly ever cried when I left him in his crib; he was so
unlike Nenad when he was little. But sometimes when Nenad
was in the room alone with him, Bozho would suddenly start
screaming. I resolved to make sure the two of them were left alone
together as little as possible, though I didn't tell Gene about any
of this. But once, when I was giving the baby a bath, I noticed a
number of small bruises on his thigh and Gene came in and saw
them too. He asked me what had caused them and I said maybe
we'd gripped him too tightly when we lifted him out of the crib.
But secretly I was sure the bruises caused by pinching and that
Nenad had been hurting Bozho whenever they were alone. I
had to be absolutely certain, though. I had to catch him in the
act. The next time I left Bozho in his crib I hid behind the wall
by the door and waited to see what would happen. Nenad was
playing on the computer. I stood there for ten minutes but nothing happened. The following day I made another attempt. This
time I spoke especially tenderly to Bozho when I put him in the

crib and deliberately didn't kiss Nenad when I left the room. I watched through the door as Nenad crept over to Bozho's crib and squeezed his little hands through the slats. Then the baby began to scream. Nenad literally didn't know what had hit him at first because I came up from behind when I delivered the blow. He fell to the floor at once, screwing up his face and beginning to wail. Both of the children were wailing now and I soon started to cry myself. I took Bozho out of the crib and grabbed Nenad by the arm. He didn't resist, maybe because it was the first time he'd seen me cry like this. We all went into the living room together and hugged and cried, and after a time we all fell asleep. Following that incident, I didn't say anything more to Nenad about not loving his brother. Something dark and heavy would rise in my chest every time I even thought about sitting him down for a talk. Usually I'd just end up kissing the back of his neck, his soft and tender nape. And I kissed and cuddled him all the more whenever Gene cooed and fussed over Bozho.

Gene was over the moon when Bozho finally found his voice and started babbling whenever he heard children's music. "Daddy's little musician!" he'd cry out happily. "Just look at him," he'd say, carried away by the baby's gurgling. "See how talented he is? How much he likes music? My sister and I have always had good voices, of course. She plays the piano better than me, I admit, but still we're both very much musically minded. Unlike you, of course," he'd say, as if playfully. "We all know you're virtually tone-deaf!" He liked to tease me, though he knew I had a complex about being unable to sing. "Our musical talent comes from my uncle Grigor," he said. "You know my uncle studied the piano in Russia, don't you? He fled during the Revolution because he was in the White Army. Aristocracy, you see. Granted he was Macedonian, but he moved in aristocratic circles. Plus he came from a rich old Skopje family. He returned to Macedonia as a top pianist, a maestro. And of course he was also strikingly tall and handsome. Just like Franz Liszt!" He often repeated this story about his uncle. Never once did I ask who Franz Liszt was, however, for fear of encouraging further descriptions of his famous Uncle Grigor. "My height and stature come from Grigor too," he added, smiling proudly. "As you know, everyone else in my family is shorter than me. I was the lucky one to have inherited the genes of such a man. It's a crying shame I never met him. I don't even have a photo of him. Oh, Grigor! Oh, Grigor! Who knows what might have been if he hadn't developed that terrible muscle atrophy." Gene would shift a little in his chair when it came to this part of his uncle's story. He was superstitious when it came talking about diseases, especially around the children. "This other one here takes after you, though," he'd say, nodding toward Nenad but talking about the child as if he wasn't right there in front of him. "Not the least bit musical," he would say of Nenad in front of him. Nenad wouldn't make any reaction to such remarks and pretended he wasn't even listening. And then I'd kiss him out of pity because I knew he really was listening and keenly felt his father's dismissal of him as "this other one here." He was a sensitive and highly intelligent boy.

That's why I was so sure he would do well at elementary school, which in fact he did. He was the best student in his class, and even in the first few months the teachers told us he was "inquisitive" and "hardworking." They didn't say he was exceptional, though. When they spoke about him it was always in a formal way, full of stock phrases they repeat about all children: "excellent grades," "shows curiosity," and "finishes his tasks in a timely manner." The only thing singled out about our boy was his "above-average success." But I sensed no warmth in their words, and when I asked them about his character they told me he was "withdrawn" and "insufficiently socialized," but that this was "quite normal" for children in the first grade.

Sometime later, though, the school hauled us in for a meeting. They called Gene's cellphone and said we needed to come in to speak to the school counsellor the following morning about a matter that could not be discussed over the phone. Gene's face was gray when he told me why the school had phoned. He yelled out to Nenad to come into the living room. "Let's ask him what this is all about," he said. Nenad shuffled in and stood before us staring at the ground, his mouth twisted into a little smile.

"What did you do at school today?" demanded Gene. His

anger was evident. We'd agreed beforehand that he'd play the bad cop, I the good cop, "in order to maintain clear family boundaries." Nenad was silent, drawing imaginary circles on the floor with his left foot.

"Answer me when I speak to you!" yelled Gene.

Nenad looked his father in the eye, defiant and without shame.

"Nothing," he said.

"Well how come they've just phoned to ask us to come to the school tomorrow, eh?"

"I don't know," said Nenad, his defiance weakening a little. He raised his eyebrows pleadingly and his eyes filled with tears. "I don't know," he repeated, doing his best to look innocent and vulnerable.

"You didn't steal anything again, did you?" asked Gene, his tone softening slightly too.

"No I didn't steal anything!" said Nenad, and a teardrop rolled down his cheek. He wasn't really crying, though, just welling up.

"Because you know where thieves end up, don't you?" said Gene, standing over the boy and looking him straight in the eyes. "I'll tell you where," he added, leaning to whisper in Nenad's ear, "in *jail*."

Nenad burst into tears. "I don't want to go to jai-i-i-l," he sobbed, choking on his tears. "Don't put me in jai-i-i-l." His pleading and wailing went on for a whole hour before he finally calmed down.

"He's stealing again," said Gene that night when we were in bed. "Otherwise he wouldn't have reacted that way."

"Maybe we punished him too hard over that car."

"And if we hadn't? You know as well as I do that he'd be stealing whenever he got the chance. We have to put the fear of God into him! It's an instinct, a pathological one. A genetic trait." He turned to the other side of the bed and I stared at the ceiling, feeling guilty for passing my bad genes on to Nenad. I've stolen things too, just like my grandfather. And now my son is also stealing, I thought to myself and welled up with tears, struggling not to cry in front of Gene.

But it wasn't because Nenad had been stealing that they'd called us to his school. It was something worse. As soon as we arrived, the counselor told us that Nenad had "acted aggressively" toward one of his classmates the previous day. This classmate, the counselor told us, was "a vulnerable, sensitive child," picked on by the other children because of his "physical disabilities" and "probably also his ethnic background."

"What 'ethnic background' are you referring to?" asked Gene. My husband seemed remarkably self-assured as he sat there, leaning back in his chair with his legs stretched out and his feet casually crossed. It wasn't genuine though. I'd seen him secretly knock back a couple of Diazepam just before we left home. He was overdressed and he'd sprayed on too much cologne. His expensive gray suit looked flashy and out of place amongst the battered old furniture of the counselor's office, lined wall to wall with dusty cabinets holding sets of Serbian and Russian books that had never been opened and never would be.

"The child is of Albanian background," the counselor said.

"Aha," Gene cried, as if he'd caught her out. "I must confess, I didn't know this neighborhood was inhabited by Sh—"

I cut him off just as he was about to use the derogatory word for Albanians.

"What exactly is it that Nenad did?"

"He locked Shkodran in the cleaners' storeroom," the counselor said.

"In a closet, you mean," I said, breaking into a sudden sweat.

"'Shkodran'?" Gene repeated the name, jutting out his chin and deliberately raising his eyebrows.

"Something like that," the counselor replied, addressing me and not paying any attention to Gene. "The storeroom is in a separate building from the school and I'm afraid Shkodran spent more than two whole hours in there. No one could hear his cries for help because it's so far from the other rooms. The poor child was terrified. He has a speech impediment already, you see—I mean he stutters—" the counselor said, but Gene cut her off.

"And how exactly did Nenad manage, as you claim, to procure a key to the storeroom?" Gene interrupted, adopting a formal tone now as if he was somehow conducting this interview. "And what were the cleaners doing for these two hours? It seems to me that some people might not be doing their jobs properly around here!" I flushed from head to toe with embarrassment and shame.

The counselor sat up straight in her chair. "Sir, the fact that the cleaners didn't go to the storeroom has nothing whatsoever to do with what happened. Somehow Nenad managed to get hold of the key. We don't know how, but he probably stole it from one of the cleaners without her realizing it. Shkodran wasn't able to tell us any details, you see. He couldn't stop stuttering when we got him out. He was locked in there for so long he still hasn't fully recovered, I'm afraid."

For a few moments, we sat there without saying a word.

"What's important for the time being," said the counselor at last, "is that you have a talk with your son and find out what prompted him to do such a thing."

"I just don't know!" I said. "I really don't know what this is all about!" A bead of sweat rolled from my armpit to my waist. "He's not an aggressive child," I lied.

"I sincerely hope there's no ethnic basis to this aggression," the counselor went on, as though she hadn't heard my words at all. "We're all equal in the eyes of God," she added, glancing at an icon of the Virgin Mary propped on her desk among her pencils and pens. "I hope we won't have cause to report this as a case of ethnic hatred." She blinked repeatedly as she waited for a response, but Gene kept quiet.

"Absolutely not!" I protested. She spoke to us as if she were addressing a press conference. There was no warmth in her words, and quite possibly no genuine concern at all.

"Of course it's unlikely that your son's actions were motivated by ethnic hatred," she said. "It's more likely that Nenad has fallen under the influence of certain classmates who cannot embrace diversity. All the same," she added, lowering her voice and looking directly at Gene, "we must always bear in mind that intolerance is most commonly fomented in the home environment."

Gene listened with affected indifference.

"Often these kinds of problems . . . problems of socialization, I mean," she went on in her officious style, "are intrinsically connected, as I have already said, with the home environment. Exposure to physical violence, for example, or the infliction of corporal punishment can have severely detrimental—"

"Madam," Gene snapped, clenching his jaw in his effort to control his rage. "Are you by any chance implying that I beat my wife?" The counselor was about to object but Gene spoke over her. "Are you suggesting I beat my child? That I 'inflict corporal punishment,' as you so ridiculously put it? Well, let me inform you right now that we are a decent, functional, and respectable family. Our children have never been stinted love and attention. Not once!" he said, beginning to yell. "Unlike ninety-nine per cent of the children in this shambolic, filthy place you call a school. And let me tell you this!" he thundered, banging his fists on the armrests of the chair, "We had *no* problems with our child, absolutely *none*, until the day he started coming here. So what do you think about that? Who's really to blame here?"

"Sir . . ." protested the counselor.

"No! That's it! I don't want to hear another word from so-called professionals like yourself. I'll talk to my son at home. *Your* job is to deal with him while he's here and find out what provoked my son—to ascertain precisely *why* he shut this Shonky character in the closet."

"Shkodran," the counselor corrected him.

The veins in Gene's temples were bulging now. I reached over to touch his shoulder, worried something even worse might happen.

"We're leaving," he said, grabbing my arm, and stalked out of the office, dragging me with him. The way to the exit seemed at least a mile long. In our anger we'd taken a wrong turn and ended up in front of a locked gate before having to circle all the way back past the counselor's office, though luckily her door was closed. We said nothing to each other the whole way home. When we got back, I dashed inside to tend to Bozho, while Gene went off to work.

When he came home later that day, he played only with the

baby and ignored our elder son completely. Nenad was alone
in his bedroom. He didn't come out at all. Watching Bozho
laughing with his father, listening to him breathing calmly as
he nodded off, all the stress and pain I felt over Nenad began to
drain away. This baby won't grow up to be like him, I thought,
instantly feeling awful for thinking such a thing.

"Daddy's little star!" Gene was now cooing over Bozho. "Your
Daddy's pride and joy! The best little baby in the whole wide
world!" He'd never said such things to Nenad.

I asked him what we were going to do about the boy. "I can't
deal with it now. I can't think straight. I need some time to mull
it over."

Then the phone rang and everything changed. "All bad things
come at once," my grandmother used to say, and nobody knew
more about "bad things" than her. It was Vaska, Gene's sister. She
was calling to give him the news that their mother had died of
a heart attack. Gene wept like a little boy. After the call, he shut
himself away in the bedroom and cried for a whole hour. Then
he left and didn't come home until the following day.

In the week after the funeral Gene talked about his mother
constantly. About what a great martyr she'd been, bringing up
her family after being widowed so young. How she'd brought her
children up with *honor* and *dignity*. What a model *housewife* she'd
been and yet, at the same time, how *professional* and *conscientious*
she'd been in her job as a history teacher. How *extensive* her knowledge of history was and how it was she who'd taught him "the
truth" about Macedonia and our noble origins. In all these lamen-
tations Gene never once mentioned how his mother had referred
to myself and my brother as *paupers*. Or the many times she'd
told me, even when I was actually pregnant with Nenad, that I'd
never give birth to a male child. Nor how his mother had signed
over the family's holiday house to Vaska when all she'd ever given
us was an old washing machine. How she'd never once invited
us all to dinner after I gave birth, but insisted on Gene going
there for dinner by himself every Saturday. Nor did she mention
how, once, when she was renovating her apartment and stayed
at our place for a fortnight, she had forced me to wash her feet.

Vaska was her favorite and the one who actually looked like her. The one who'd inherited her genes. Infinitely selfish and vain, Vaska frittered away her time on elaborate beauty treatments and refining her affected aristocratic manner. Otherwise she was just an empty shell. Only her eyes were animate, literally gleaming with malice.

That same malice glistened in Vaska's eyes when she sat down at the kitchen table with Gene to discuss the estate after their mother's death. I sat with them to lend my husband support, partly because I had a feeling something underhand would happen, but also just to annoy her. There was no one to support Vaska. She was a divorcee. No man could possibly have put up with her.

Seated opposite us she plucked a piece of paper out of her purse and placed it on the table in front of Gene. It was a detailed list, penned in her own hand with different colored highlighting and multiple revisions. The more I tried to make sense of it the more it was clear that this was a ledger of pure evil.

The list was in tabular form, with columns for each year and rows labelled "items," "amounts" and "assets." In the spaces between the intersecting horizontal and vertical lines, she had entered the full forms of their two names—Vasilia and Eugene—hers highlighted in green and his in yellow. The yellow actually predominated, but neither Gene nor I could even recognize the items, amounts, and assets highlighted. There were only a few entries highlighted in green, and the holiday house was nowhere to be seen. The very fact she had drawn up this ledger was so appalling that we were at a loss how to react. We simply refused to accept what had been laid in front of us. It was like having to cope with the grief all over again. I squeezed Gene's knee under the table, afraid of how he might react. And as we sat there dumbstruck, Vaska "explained" the contents of the ledger.

"Maybe it's a little unclear to you now but this is the way things stand. It was Mom who originally drew up the list. I merely copied it out. She didn't draw up an official will, but she did leave this list. If you want, I can show you the original copy," she bluffed, lighting a cigarette in a holder and adopting a haughty tone. "In any case the upshot is that over the years you have accumulated property and other tangible assets amounting to more than half the value of the apartment, which she left to us both." Vaska crossed herself when she mentioned her mother, though she wasn't in the slightest religious.

"I beg your pardon?" Gene said. A crease had formed between his eyebrows, a crease I'd never seen before. The corners of his lips were turned down as if he were about to cry.

"Here, read this part. Everything's worked out and written down," said Vaska, tapping a red fingernail at a corner of the page where she had scrawled some sinister calculation of totals alongside their two names, with her own name underlined.

"What is all this nonsense? Have you gone crazy?" Gene asked, with the same new crease between his eyebrows.

"Don't insult me."

"Don't *you* insult me."

"Please at least try to be civil, Gene. Don't sink to this level," she pleaded, her voice beginning to falter as she abruptly switched to playing the victim. I felt like grabbing the ashtray off the table and smashing it over her head. "After all, you're still my brother," she went on, "in a way."

"In a way? What do you mean 'in a way'?" Gene asked.

"Well, since you *insist* on dragging it out of me I'll tell you what I mean. It's time you knew the truth anyway," she said, pausing dramatically to take a deep breath before going on as our anxiety mounted. "The fact is that I came here today with a mind to tell you this. Now that Mom's dead you really ought to know the truth because—well, who knows what might happen? Genes are genes, after all, and you might even now have some underlying condition you're unaware of . . . Genetic diseases can manifest themselves in all sorts of different ways . . ."

"What the hell are you talking about?" Gene snapped.

Vaska looked down at her lap and smoothed her dress before resuming, undaunted by his insolence. "I'm sure it must have crossed your mind, Gene, why there is such a gap in our ages. Well, it's not an accident. For a long time Mom and Dad didn't think they could have children. They tried for a long time and went to various doctors who told them they'd never be able to conceive. The doctors said everything appeared to be normal but something was wrong and it was not easy to diagnose what that something was. So they decided to adopt a child. That's how they got you. From an orphanage. You were six months old."

"Vaska," I interrupted. "Please stop talking nonsense."

"You stay out of this," she snapped. "This is a private conversation between me and Gene." Gene sat with his head in his hands. His eyes were fixed on Vaska but it was as if he didn't really see her. As if he could no longer focus. "Anyway, after a long time their luck finally changed," Vaska went on. "And I was born. 'Like a miracle,' Mom said."

Vaska smiled slightly to herself and smoothed her dress again as we stared at her in silence.

"You had another name, but they changed it and gave you this one."

"What was I called?" Gene asked and I realized he was beginning to believe her.

"I don't know. You'd need to see the adoption certificate. It's in Mom's safety deposit box at the bank. I can make an appointment for you if you want. We can go this week and you can have a look to see for yourself," she said. And placing her hand on her heart she added, "That way you can confirm that every single word I've told you tonight is the absolute truth." Her mission accomplished, Vaska leaned her head back with her nose in the air and closed her eyes.

A wave of hatred washed over me. Gene sat there in silence, his hands clasped tight in a way that was unlike him. Then his shoulders slumped and he bowed his head. Vaska reached over the table to take his hands in hers, feigning sympathy. But her skin looked as cold and clammy as a snake's and I didn't want her to touch Gene. The veins at his temples were throbbing. Usually his face grew red when this happened, but now he had turned frighteningly pale. I left the table to pour him a glass of water and Vaska leaned in closer to him, her wrists and hands clustered with bangles and rings. "I know all this must be difficult for you," she said, "I mean, learning that you're not of the same blood as us."

At that point I knew I had to kick her out of our house. "Out!" I ordered her. "Now! Take your bag and go!" Vaska's jaw dropped in shock. "Disgraceful behavior!" she cried as I bustled her out of the door. "I've never experienced such crude manners in my life!" she protested. "Gene, be reasonable! We did grow up together after all." But I wasn't going to listen to her any more and slammed the door, not sorry in the least for insulting her.

Gene fell into a terrible state over the following days. He looked utterly drained, as if voided on the inside. He'd stare vacantly into the distance or go into the bathroom and stare at himself in the mirror for a long time. He took out the old family album and studied the faces of everyone in his family for hours. He prodded his cheeks, his eyebrows; he pulled at his earlobes when he thought I wasn't looking. On the third day after Vaska's visit, a colleague from Gene's office phoned to inform me that my husband had suffered a stroke. They gave me the name of the hospital ward and told me Gene was in a "stable condition."

When I got to the hospital, he was asleep. He was in a ward with three other male patients who seemed completely motionless. Their loved ones sat around their beds speaking in hushed voices as if at a funeral. Some straightened the sheets or laid out food on trays and arranged flowers in vases on the bedside tables. But Gene's tray was empty and there was nothing on his table. I felt miserable for having come there alone and empty-handed.

When Gene woke up I saw the right side of his face was drooping. He spoke slowly, as if his mouth was filled with soggy bread. He was trying desperately to tell me how he loved me and was struggling not to cry. I took his right hand, the one that was now almost motionless, and kissed it for a long time. I kissed his face and his neck and the Adam's apple I loved so much. His beard scratched me and I enjoyed the way it felt against my skin. I told him how much I loved him and that he would soon come home and everything would be all right. Later as I was leaving he held on to my hand. "Bring Nenad!" he said, "I really want to see him. And bring me one of those chocolate bars with almonds." Gene loved chocolate with almonds. It was his favorite kind, whereas Nenad particularly despised that kind of chocolate and claimed it made him sick. When he was younger he would cry whenever he emptied the candy jar and found the only bars left were almond chocolate.

I brought Nenad with me the next day, even though I was wary of exposing him to the dreadful smell of death and decay that lingered throughout the hospital. Nor did I want him to see the other patients in Gene's ward or the plastic plates they had to eat from and the prison-like bars on the sides of their beds. Most of all I worried how he would react to seeing his father lying there in yellowed sheets. But Nenad is strong, I told myself, He'll cope. And since Gene had specifically asked me to bring him it must be something that mattered to him a great deal. Maybe Gene will finally feel sorry for not having loved Nenad enough? I wondered, and instantly felt guilty for thinking such a thought.

Gene was asleep again when we got there. I placed some orange juice, Turkish delight, and the almond chocolate on the tray beside him. I took his hand, but he didn't wake up. I squeezed it, but that didn't wake him either. He was breathing. I had to wake him because I didn't want Nenad to think, even for a minute, that Gene had died. I shook him, and Gene opened his eyes. "Son," he said when he saw Nenad. "How are you doing my boy?" he asked. Gene hadn't called him "my boy" in a long time. That's what he called Bozho now. Nenad stared at his father expressionlessly and just shrugged. "I'm good." "Tell me something about school," Gene said, speaking with difficulty. "Did you get any more A's?" "I always get A's," Nenad replied, pulling at a thread on his sleeve. I patted the boy's head and ruffled his hair. We were sitting on the right-hand side of the bed, the side on which Gene couldn't move. "Come over to this side, son," Gene said, unable to move his hand on the right side where we were sitting. Nenad didn't budge from his spot. "Go on," I said, nudging him, and he got up and stood by his father on the other side of the bed, stiff as a statue. "Come closer, son, let me give you a kiss," Gene said, and pulled Nenad toward him. Nenad let his father wrap his arm around him and pull him close. I saw him screw up his face as if he'd smelled something bad but he stayed there pressed against his father's neck and cheek because Gene clutched him so tightly with his left arm. And when at last he did let the boy stand up he still held onto Nenad's hand, saying "You're Daddy's pride and joy, my son! You know that, don't you?" Nenad said nothing. Not even his expression changed. I leaned over from the other side and hugged Gene. His breath smelled stale as I kissed him goodbye.

Leading Nenad out of the hospital, the expressions on the faces of the people we passed all seemed ones of despair or bravado. Empty plastic yoghurt tubs and cheap junk-food wrappers lay strewn across the lawn outside. Everything reeked of illness and fried food. On the right as we walked through the main gate of the medical center we passed a *burek* stand with a long line of people waiting to be served. Nenad asked me to buy him a sesame bagel and so we joined the line, jostling like the others to get to the front. As I was rummaging through my purse for change I stumbled and dropped a five-denar coin that rolled across the sidewalk to the curb. "Get it for me, can you love?" I said. Nenad went to pick up the coin, and as he knelt to reach for it I saw the almond chocolate bar I'd bought for Gene fall out of his trouser pocket. He snatched the bar up and stuffed it back in his pocket before standing up and handing me the coin, with a conniving, impudent look that gleamed with malice, just like the glint in Vaska's eyes.

Nectar

ALTHOUGH HE'S A gynecologist, my husband tries to make out he's an artist. And that's not the only thing about him that annoys me. Actually, I don't remember when he started getting on my nerves, but I can single out this as one of the more irritating things: when we have people over he'll say he's not "a real artist" only "a dabbler in art," but that's just him pretending to be modest. And we have people over all the time, which I really dread, because it means loads of cooking and cleaning. My husband always insists on our throwing a lavish banquet, you know, to show that we're a so-called functional family. These lavish banquets are normally held in our living room, on the low table with seating for four others besides us. Since he always leaves everything to me, I'm usually stuck in the kitchen. When I finally get a chance to join the conversations, I have to sit on a stool. I always lie through my teeth whenever anyone says, "Are you comfortable?" Meanwhile, my husband just blathers on, mainly about himself. And because it's rude to talk about pussies—the only subject about which he knows a thing or two—he goes on and on about his "art," which is to say, his oil paintings. He works on them in one of the rooms in our apartment, his "studio." And this means our two boys, who are always bickering, are forced to share a single room. His paintings are amateurish, the colors blurred, dull, and depressing. Every time he makes a mistake, he slaps on a new coat of paint until they wind up looking like huge piles of vomit—like someone threw up after gorging themselves. He has the notion

his paintings are "abstract," that they "render emotional states of
anxiety and exultation." The truth is they're just pictures of the
things he knows best: pussies, from the inside and the outside. I
assume that other people—at least the more intelligent ones—can
see this too. I'm almost certain they refer to him as "the gynecologist who paints pussies," and laugh at him behind his back.
What's more, he totally deserves it. I wouldn't be the least bit
upset if that were the case. Although to his face, they flatter him.
"But you're a real artist," they say to him, staring at the paintings
as if standing before a canvas by Leonardo. That's when he pulls
out his well-worn phrase: "No, I merely dabble in art," once again
adding with false modesty, "I'm just a plain old doctor," knowing
full well the kind of status his profession enjoys.

His second big topic of conversation is, of course, his patients
and their health problems. My husband, it's worth mentioning,
has lost those friends who are outside of his profession. All his
friends are also doctors, whom he met at university, and whose
wives have now become his patients. Together they form a "boys'
club." From today's perspective, boys' clubs seem really funny to
me. When I was young, when my husband and I first met, I
thought it sweet that he had such faithful friends. But at the time,
what they discussed among themselves wasn't obvious to me. Even
less so what they said about us, their wives. And I think that my
husband is the biggest culprit among them, mainly because of
his status as a gynecologist and his knowledge of the intimate
details of all the wives. Unfortunately, I have a terrible, sinking
suspicion, which I'm afraid to put into words, that his friends
deliberately take their wives to see my husband, because thereby
they have control over them. If one of his friends contracts a
sexually transmitted disease, my husband can keep the secret. If
"the guilty party" is the wife, then he can inform his friend before
she has the chance to do so herself, or not, as the case may be.
This is just a suspicion on my part, because this boys' club—this
tribe—claims that their brotherhood is "transcends everything
else," and that they would do literally anything for each other.
Sometimes I think they're gay. That if we weren't around, and
if there were no social restraints, they'd form a line and get off

with each other. That's how I imagine them sometimes, when they get on my nerves: squashed together like sardines in a tin, or lined up like train cars, moving to the same rhythm. The only member of the tribe who'd feel shortchanged, who wouldn't get to do anything with his dick, would be the one at the head of the line. In my fantasies, we women sit on the side lines and watch. As we do in real life. They talk while we watch, or sometimes we whisper recipes to each other, when we get bored of their conversation. Sometimes the wives also manage secretly to exchange a few words with my husband in our hallway, as an additional consultation regarding their health. "Take a dose of Betadine," I overhear, or "Maybe it's my diet, I don't know why it keeps reoccurring." "Don't go on any diets." "But I eat properly. And I don't even smoke anymore."

He and I met at the gynecological examination table, when I went to see him for a checkup. He was exceptionally kind and gentle, and his technique impressed me. I was very, very young—which should be taken into account. The other gynecologists I'd gone to had been incompetent, rough, unfriendly. Not that I had any kind of a problem, quite the contrary. First, he sat me down in his office. His charm and friendliness put me at ease. Soft classical music was playing in the background. He offered me some fragrant tea, which he'd already prepared. After I'd relaxed somewhat, he showed me where to get undressed: it was a lovely little dressing room, with beautiful, white fluffy slippers on the floor, and a shiny new clothes hanger holding a loose white gown that I could wear before climbing onto the examination table. When I did, he said, "Lower down, sweetie, a bit lower down, dear," and he gently squeezed my thighs to pull me down further. After that, he started talking to me as he prepared to insert the speculum, telling me that it would be uncomfortable, but that he would be gentle. He even tried to warm it up so that it wouldn't be so unpleasant for me when he stuck it in. The way he spread my labia before inserting the speculum caused something warm to stir within me. Then he looked inside me, I at his face. I thought him handsome, most handsome, the handsomest. His blue eyes looked inside me as if they were gazing at a sunset over a peaceful lake. His face bore an expression of delight. "Ah, everything's perfect. Your anatomy is flawless," he said, repeating it when he did an ultrasound of my ovaries. "You have a magnificent uterus," he said to me several times. But before doing the ultrasound, he did something that I now know he does to other women—maybe that's why he's so popular, because of the fluffy slippers, the shiny new clothes hanger, the tea, the friendliness. With his long, delicate fingers, he poked about inside me to see if I had any pain. Naturally, he apologized several times before he did it, and he explained exactly what he was going to do. While he was poking around left and right with his forefinger, with his other fingers he gently caressed my clitoris. I enjoyed it. I went back again after six months, making up some lie about internal pains. "Everything's in order, it's perfect," he said. "I've never seen such clean and flawless anatomy," he repeated, looking rapturously inside me. And so I went to him again, every six months, for a couple of years. Until one day we bumped into one another in one of the city cafés, and in a drunken state he told me that I was the most beautiful patient with the most exquisite "how can I put it . . . it begins with 'p'" that he'd ever seen before. Then he told me that after saying what he'd just said, I could no longer be his patient, but that I could be his girlfriend. And after a few months he told me that I could be his wife. I accepted. I was twenty-one years old. He was thirty-eight. I'm still his patient.

His paintings are the principal subject of quarrels, but not the principal reason for them. The reasons are varied, but here's one more example: on one occasion, my husband and I were discussing art. Of course, he sees himself as some sort of Chekhov, someone who was once a doctor, but who later became well known for what he really was—a great artist. We were discussing our favorite writers, painters, musicians, and I started talking about how much I liked the poetry of Sylvia Plath. He paused, as if something suddenly occurred to him.

"Have you noticed that all the great artists are men?" he said.

That thought had struck me before, and I experienced it as a sore point. With disappointment I told him I had.

"What do you think: why is that so?"

I mulled it over. At the time, I wasn't able to fire off the quick retort that I would give him today: that women were never afforded the opportunities to be creative. That it simply wasn't permitted, when they spent the whole day at home, wiping the shit from babies' bottoms, as I myself had done while he traveled to conferences in China, Africa, Europe, finding inspiration.

"Well . . ." I stammered, which I now deeply regret.

"It's because men are the soul, women the body. Men are creative, women are practical. Men soar, women scavenge. Women can't be artists; it's not in their nature."

I was quite offended, but I didn't know how to respond. I was twenty-four years old, if that can serve as my defense today.

"Go on, name just one great female writer. On a level with Dostoevsky, Chekhov, and Hemingway, for example," he said.

"Well, Marguerite Yourcenar," I said, because only she came to mind at that moment.

"She doesn't count. She was a lesbian," he said, and went off to the toilet to take a crap. I knew he would be in there for quite some time. I had to go pick up our son from kindergarten and we never finished the conversation. Or else I would have rattled off the names of hundreds of gay male artists, such as his beloved composer, Tchaikovsky, for example.

His ideas about the greatness of being an artist, coupled with his own desire to become one, surfaced long ago, but he only started painting much later, after he "found himself," as he put it. Actually, he started painting intensively after our second son was born, that is, eight years ago. By then I could barely tolerate him and I'd stopped being so afraid. When he first started painting, inured to singing his praises, I would tell him that his paintings were really good and that he had true talent. His face flushed with joy whenever I said those kinds of things and he would get all emotional, swallowing hard repeatedly or looking as if he might burst into tears as he gazed at his finished canvas. "I've always wanted to be a painter!" he'd say. "I was torn between medicine and art. But my father didn't force me to follow in his footsteps.

And behold—destiny," he repeated reverently. It surprised me that he spoke like that to me, his wife, before whom he didn't have to pretend.

After that I just ignored his paintings, and finally, a couple of years ago, I took to telling him I didn't like them at all. The last time we fought, in a moment of rage, I told him they looked like ugly, smeary vaginas, and when they didn't, they were like omelets or puddles of vomit. He was deeply offended.

"At least I create," he said to me.

"Your asshole creates too," I shot back.

He was furious. The blood rushed to his face. But trained in the ability to remain self-controlled, he swallowed his rage and his face regained its normal composure after a few seconds.

"You're quite the wit today," he said, pausing, planning his attack. "It's a shame you're not a writer," he said, knowing full well that I've always wanted to write. He could see I was getting upset, so he pressed further.

"Oh! I forgot you write poetry. Why don't you read me one of your little rhymes so that I can have the pleasure of being a critic, too?" he reproached me pointedly, grinning with triumph. I'd never shown him any of my poems before but I no longer wanted to hide them. I went into the bedroom, and from under the bed, I pulled out the sheets of paper on which I secretly wrote my poems when he was at work. I gave him my most recent poem. I asked him to read it aloud.

Beloved
This night he lies beside me
while I dream of you
your nocturnal rose
opening its petals for me
as you moan like the wind
o my beloved flower
a cup of your secret nectar
I'd drink in this hour

My husband's jaws clenched as if he were grinding his teeth. His eyes flared as he glared at me. His face had grown pale.

"It doesn't exactly rhyme," I said to him cynically. "Sorry to have disappointed you."

"No," he answered, "I'm not disappointed. I expected it to be shit."

Empty Nest

I'VE ALWAYS BEEN good at painting. I'm creative in other areas, too, but it's painting that attracts me the most. Even at elementary school I was good at art and won several prizes for my work. But then I went to a high school for medical students, and later, after getting a job and meeting my husband, I gave birth to my two kids and didn't have time for painting anymore. So I never really mastered it. But now the kids have left home, I can devote myself to painting full-time. I'm making rapid progress and have dramatically improved. I'm definitely no longer an amateur.

Probably it's because I never completely neglected my talent even when my whole life revolved around the kids. Before they started school, I bought them all sorts of crayons and sketch pads and plasticine, and tried to pass on some of my skills. Unfortunately these don't include a talent for sculpture, as I soon found out in my attempts with plasticine. Once, for example, I sculpted a small elephant for my son but when I showed it to him he couldn't tell it was an elephant and insisted on calling it a dog. That stung me a bit, even if it was only a child's opinion. And when I explained to him that it wasn't a dog but an elephant, pointing out its trunk and large ears, he burst into tears. I never had much success with my daughter either. She had a bad habit of pulling apart and squashing my plasticine sculptures, which really hurt my feelings. Sadly, all my attempts at stimulating their creativity from preschool age came to nothing. They simply haven't inherited my artistic talent. That's why I always helped them out with their school art projects. Besides, it helped keep me in form, and helping them with their art was the only "free" time I had when I could do something for them—always my main priority—while also doing something I enjoyed. Sometimes, I must admit, I ended up completing their art homework assignments entirely by myself. But all my efforts blew up in my face one day as my daughter was finishing elementary school.

Whenever I remember what happened that day I well up with anger and shame, and I get a strong urge to break something, though usually I manage to restrain myself. I still don't know how I managed to stop myself from grabbing that teacher by her greasy red ponytail and slapping her about the head. Instead, I snatched a sketchpad and flung it across the classroom. It made such a loud noise as it clattered across the green linoleum floor that the teacher jumped back in shock. She was even more alarmed by my next move, however, as I grabbed a paint-splattered jug full of brushes and tubes and hurled it to the floor with all my might, smashing it to pieces. A shard flew to the opposite end of the classroom and the brushes and tubes scattered all over the floor, some of them rolling underneath a radiator where years of dust and grime had gathered.

"Drunk again?" said my husband later that day. It's typical of him to turn it back on me. It's not true I was drunk, and if for once he himself had managed to stay sober when he wasn't at work, I'm quite sure he'd have been just as angry as I was at the teacher for giving our daughter a B. On top of it all, my daughter had delivered the news of her humiliating grade with such perverse delight. I decided at once to go over to the school the next day and confront the teacher during the lunchbreak.

The following morning I got up early so that I'd have time to go to the hairdresser's. I put on a new suit and applied some tasteful makeup. I stopped to look at myself in the hall mirror before I left. I liked what I saw. I looked smart and fresh and crisp. I wanted to look confident and strong, which is how I normally feel in fact.

When I got to the school, I marched straight to the teachers' common room. It didn't take long at all to find her. It was obvious at once which one she was: the shabbiest-looking of the lot, dripping in tacky dime-store jewelry and with long unwashed hair, dyed bright orange like the paintwork on a cheap 1970s car. The "arty" one, in other words. She was thin as a rake, of course, her boobs sagging braless under a lace-sleeved top. I went up to her and asked if we could have a talk about my daughter's grades. She led me out of the common room and ushered me into her empty classroom where, shortly thereafter, I was to hurl the sketchpad across the room and smash the jug full of brushes and tubes of paint.

I challenged her immediately as to why she'd given my daughter only a B for such a good still life. I asked her if she was aware how much time and effort my daughter had put into the painting and how expensive the materials were. But the teacher just nodded her head as I talked, gazing at me with her amber eyes, daubed with cheap eyeliner that had started to clump and flake under her lower eyelashes. And when I'd finished, she replied— in the rudest possible way—that while she valued my daughter's efforts in class, she had given her a B because the painting wasn't her own work.

I made a snap decision to double down hard. I realize it wasn't entirely ethical on my part, but having come this far, I couldn't very well turn back now. I told her these accusations were *absurd, ignorant* and *extremely offensive.* Yes, I conceded, I may have given my daughter a helping hand with the still life, though only by *suggesting* how to go about it, helping her with certain strokes and so on. But that was only natural given that I am, after all, something of a painter myself and know a few tricks unlikely to be familiar to amateurs. Nonetheless, I repeatedly and emphatically rejected the allegation that the still life was not my daughter's own work. The accusation was utterly baseless. And what was more, I added, she simply had no way of proving it.

"But I can prove it," she said, without her face seeming to move a single muscle. "I'll just ask her to do another painting of a pomegranate in class. The B is for the person who painted this one, not for your daughter."

That was when I flew into a rage. I still get angry now when

I think of her saying those words to me. It makes me want to smash her bony face to smithereens.

Of course, my husband blamed it all on me as usual, accusing me of always ruining everything. According to him, I was the main cause of all the problems in our marriage and with the children, whereas he was busy day and night *making connections with the right people* that would move us up in the world. And here I was coming home to him after yet another *disgraceful drunken outburst*, as he called it, which deeply offended me. His breath reeked of alcohol as he said it, too, which infuriated me even more, and I informed him of it right there and then. That night we had a huge fight and the windows in the bedroom and his study ended up getting smashed.

After that incident I stopped helping the kids with their painting. Besides, before long they stopped having art classes at school. Time was passing and I wasn't getting anywhere in my efforts to improve my painting technique. But at least I still had my creativity, and I resolved to channel my talents into the garden. Even back then we could have afforded to hire a gardener, but I decided to design and maintain the garden myself. It also helped me stay in shape, which was no small incentive now that my body had suddenly sagged, as if overnight, like worn-out elastic. Not only did I arrange the flowers and plants and tend them, but also, I added some striking stone borders around the roses and the other flowerbeds. Soon I started making sculptures and small water features to place among the flowers. I loved showing them off to guests and it gave me great satisfaction whenever someone praised my work. It really was a unique-looking garden, a work of singular creativity that I had made entirely by myself, giving free rein to my vivid imagination and artistic talent. What wounded me, however, was that no one in my family either acknowledged it or gave me any credit for the work I'd done. In her typical fashion, my daughter just scoffed at me. She told me I should be doing something more worthwhile than wasting my time on something we could get a gardener to do "professionally." She even claimed I'd been "harassing" our guests with my "tiresome" garden when the truth was that no one was remotely interested in hearing about my "boring" stone borders. My son was there listening as my daughter laid into me, something she most probably did out of jealousy, since, although she feels the need to compete with me, she herself is not creative. In fact she's quite remarkably ignorant and narrow-minded, and of course there's also the matter of her not having turned out as attractive as I am. My son told her *to stop talking crap.* But he's a coward in his own way and only says what he thinks will make him look good in front of other people, never what he really thinks. My husband, on the other hand, just tells me not to worry, saying *enjoy yourself and do whatever makes you feel fulfilled,* which frankly sounds even worse, as if my art were just a meaningless distraction, unlike his squash-playing, which he treats as if each game is a serious endeavor. The squash court is where he "networks" with all his managerial buddies. They all go out together afterward to eat and drink and they come home late stinking of sweat and garlic and alcohol.

But I refused to let any of this discourage me. The children eventually left home and suddenly I had all this time on my hands, enough time to design and maintain a hundred gardens. And the more time I spent among my flowers, the more I was inspired to paint *en plein air.* Like the celebrated Monet, I too came to find that painting outdoors—capturing the varying tones and colors of natural sunlight that change by the hour—is the only true way to paint. Those who don't understand painting cannot understand how much more difficult this is than painting in a studio. Of course I have a studio at home now—in my daughter's old bedroom—but painting *en plein air* is a much bigger challenge. The light shifts as the sun moves in and out of the clouds, and as it does so the concept behind the painting changes constantly too. Realism is not my priority. To be sure, I want people to recognize the object as a petunia, a gardenia, a chrysanthemum or a gerbera, but realism is not the main goal. Sometimes I put together different flowers in the same bouquet, even though they don't actually grow next to each other in the garden. I allow myself a lot of artistic freedom, which I find immensely fulfilling.

It was partly my love of painting and my desire to share

it with others that persuaded me to invite my niece to come and stay with us. I'd initially had reservations, since whenever she'd visited before, she'd always seemed somewhat troubled and neglected. But then again, her folks weren't doing too well financially and I felt a certain responsibility toward her and her family, because her grandfather had helped me so much when I was younger. As I wanted to repay the debt somehow, I decided to take her in during her final year at university, so that she wouldn't have to pay for board and lodgings elsewhere. She's studying painting and sometimes takes on graphic design jobs to earn a bit of money on the side. Maybe I'll find a kindred spirit, I said to myself, and finally have someone to talk to about my paintings. But in this I was sorely mistaken.

For a start, I thought she'd at least pay a bit more attention to my paintings and want to discuss them with me at length. But it was as if she refused to leave her room whenever I was painting in the garden. She'd shut herself inside for hours on end, "working" on her computer. She only painted in the studios at the university, even though I offered to share mine with her or let her work in the house. And whenever she did walk past me in the garden while I was painting, which happened only if she couldn't avoid it, she wouldn't say hello but just nod and smile politely. To me that was a clear sign that things weren't quite right between us.

The second sign that we weren't going to get on well and that I'd made a mistake by inviting her to live with us was the patronizing way she'd respond to my paintings on the rare occasions she noticed them at all. "Well done!" she said, the first time I showed her my work. "That's great! I'm really glad you're painting!" As if I were a small child. Her words and her condescending tone cut me to the quick. Later, however, I invited her into my studio and showed her the works for the exhibition I was planning. The exhibition was called *Le Quattro Stagioni*, after Vivaldi's famous violin concerti. I'd painted plants and flowers from the garden from each season of the year and displayed them according to the four seasons. Naturally, I didn't have so many paintings for winter, since there aren't any flowers out then, so instead I painted bare branches and evergreen shrubs covered in snow. Naturally, it was my *Spring* and *Summer* cycles that were the most abundant. We stood in front of the paintings and I explained the concept behind the exhibition. "I think it's quite an original idea, don't you?" I said, disconcerted by her silence and the way she just stared at each painting with the same polite but wooden smile. "Yes, indeed," she nodded, and started asking me what kind of oils I used, where I bought my canvases, and other technical questions that had nothing to do with the paintings. She did eventually deign to comment on a few details here and there. "The use of color here is quite rich . . . Ah, this really is a quite unique-looking flower! . . . This one is very expressive . . ." But not once did she actually say she *liked* my work or even say how *pretty* it was. Actually, she did remark that one thing was "pretty"—the picture frames. My husband had bought them for me. He has good taste when it comes to those kinds of things. He's also good at interior design. He was the one who furnished and decorated the whole house. So, he chose the frames. "They were quite expensive," I replied. "I know," she said. And that's how our little private viewing of my exhibition ended.

Time passed, but my anger toward my niece did not abate. She continued to ignore my art and seemed oblivious to the fact that she was living in the home of another, more mature artist. I began to believe it was because she saw me as a rival. She didn't want to open herself up to my energy—to feel the sincerity and warmth of what I was doing and take in the beauty of the world through my paintings. Instead, she shrouded herself in ugliness through her own "art." These efforts of hers invariably depicted gaunt female nudes, screaming or crying and clutching at their necks and their sparse clumps of hair, all painted in black and white with red tints. They reminded me a bit of that Munch painting, *The Scream*. In some of them you couldn't tell if the subjects were really women or just weird-looking creatures. Those that were definitely intended to be women had withered and sagging breasts like you see in pictures of elderly African women. Some had just one breast while others had had their breasts cut off. Some had ugly, plucked wings. I shuddered whenever I looked at her work. They looked like something you'd only ever see in a nightmare. "Very interesting," I said, the first time she showed me them, smiling politely at her the same way she'd smiled at me when she'd viewed the paintings for my exhibition.

I also sensed a rivalry between us in the manner in which she had started behaving toward my husband. Whenever she saw him she'd start to laugh, opening her mouth so wide you could see all of her teeth. Her whole body would instantly take on a different posture and she would start acting a bit boyishly, slouching with her hands in her pockets and swinging her elbows about when she spoke. I noticed how my husband responded to her as well. He too laughed a lot. They even laughed loudly together. I'd be working in the garden and, all of a sudden, I'd hear a burst of raucous double-barreled laughter coming from inside the house. I'd go in and find them sitting at the kitchen counter, drinking wine and sharing anecdotes with each other, but the fun would stop the moment I walked in. I'd try to join in and they'd even attempt to include me, but the conversation would soon just fizzle out. Sometimes I'd try joining them when they were watching a cartoon show they both liked on TV. The show had four kids in it who just cursed the whole time and beat each other up. For some reason it sent my husband and my niece into hysterics, but I found the whole thing disgusting and morbid and had no desire to waste my time watching such trash.

One night, just before we went to sleep, lying in our double bed, my husband and I had a bit of a frank chat about my niece. "I feel badly about it," I complained. "I don't think she likes me."

"Rubbish!" he said. "Not only does she like you, but also she feels very grateful and indebted to you."

"Then she doesn't show it," I said. "I don't mean she acts badly toward me exactly . . . but we can both see how much better the two of you get along."

"Well why wouldn't we? It's perfectly natural. We share the same interests. She likes to read about history. She's interested in politics. She likes satire. We have the same sense of humor . . ."

I really didn't know what to say to that. For one thing, it clearly implied that as far as my husband was concerned we didn't have the same sense of humor.

"She doesn't like my paintings," I said.

"That's not true! She's always praising your work. She thinks you should have an exhibition as soon as possible."

I went through the motions of protesting and disagreeing with him, though all I really wanted to do was just cry and lick my wounds.

"You have different sensibilities, true," he conceded.

I didn't say anything.

"But actually it's *you* who doesn't like *her* work," he said.

"I'm twice her age!" I said, bristling, "And I have substantially more experience of painting than her."

Seeing how offended I was, he held my hand and tried to calm me down.

"You shouldn't underestimate her," he said. "She's an adult, too. It's just you have different sensibilities, that's all."

He fell asleep still holding my hand, and once his breathing slowed, I fell asleep too.

After that night, I felt a little less angry with my niece and slightly more at ease. It didn't last long, however, and everything came to a head on the evening of our thirtieth wedding anniversary. We'd planned a big party, and since it was springtime and warm outside, we set up a fancy marquee in the garden. In the weeks leading up to the celebration I worked hard on the party, the garden, and myself. I wanted everything to be absolutely perfect. I injected some Botox in my forehead. I went to the gym, had body massages, and drank detoxifying tea for a whole month. I sewed myself a blue dress from raw silk that fit me like a glove. I made my husband a blue suit and a blue tie out of the same material.

I must admit my husband looks quite a lot older than me even though there's only three years between us. His aged appearance is due mostly to his baldness and his big belly, plus the double chin that he's had since he was young but which is now twice as big. He doesn't care what he looks like and he doesn't look after his health. At the party everybody said that of the two of us, it was as if he was the only one who had aged. He didn't like that, I could tell, but I also knew he was proud of the fact that his wife was still young-looking and beautiful. He put his arm around my waist and gently led me from table to table, from drinks stand to drinks stand, where we stood chatting with friends and acquaintances and my husband's work colleagues. At every table, at every drinks stand, in every corner of the garden, my husband clinked glasses with the guests. As soon as a waiter walked by, he'd help himself to a fresh glass of vodka from the tray. Noticing that my husband had developed something of a thirst, the waiter started to pass by more and more often. I poked my husband's side a few times and glared at the glass in his hand to warn him.

"Heh, heh!" he sputtered and laughed, throwing his head back the way he always does when he's drunk. "And you're sober, right?"

At which point everything started to go wrong. He started to drink more and more, almost as if he meant to spite me. He started slurring his words, and instead of holding me with his arm around my waist, he started pulling me by the belt of my dress, dragging it down. "Control yourself!" I hissed, but he just grew louder and more obnoxious. At one point he left me standing alone in the middle of the garden and disappeared somewhere. I went looking for him, but he was nowhere to be found. I went inside the house and searched through all the rooms. He wasn't there either. I asked my niece if she'd seen him. She smiled politely as usual and told me the last time she'd seen him was five minutes ago, when he was with me. It was then that it occurred to me to look for him at the back of the garden. I found him standing there, with his forehead propped against the trunk of the maple tree, holding his penis with both hands.

"I can't piss!" he moaned, shaking his hips left and right and swaying backward and forward.

I took him to the bathroom and sat him down on the toilet seat and waited for him outside, worried he might fall off and hit his head on the sink or the bath. When he finally flushed the toilet I went in and forced him to splash cold water on his face. That woke him up a bit and he appeared to be in better spirits.

We walked hand in hand back out into the garden and found the guests chatting and enjoying themselves, oblivious to everything that had gone on between us.

As soon as I let go of his hand, however, he seemed intent on causing further catastrophes. I followed closely as he lurched over to a group of our friends, including Olga and Jan, who own an art gallery.

"You know," he said, butting into their conversation and turning to give me a meaningful look, with one eye half-closed, "my wife here has been painting a lot lately."

"Yes, yes, we know, we know!" they all said, nodding approvingly and smiling politely, just like my niece.

"It's time for you to hold another exhibition!" cried out a friend of Olga and Jan's, a man I'd never seen before.

"Let's drink to that!" my husband blustered, and everyone raised their glasses. "To humanity!" he cried out, at which everyone stared at him strangely, their glasses held mid-air. "To my wife's humanitarian exhibition!" he hollered even louder, at which everyone relaxed a little and clinked glasses. They were all smiles after that, which really annoyed me.

"What's this about an exhibition?" asked my niece, appearing out of nowhere.

"We're going to organize a humanitarian exhibition for your aunt," said Olga, nodding toward me.

"That's wonderful news," said my niece, in that same formal, polite tone she always uses.

"Ah so that's where the niece's artistic genes come from!" said Jan loudly, looking at my niece. She smiled shyly and took a sip of her vodka.

"Wonderful, wonderful!" my husband nodded with his eyes closed and the corners of his mouth turned down. "Exceptional talent. She has great artistic vision."

My niece looked down at her shoes, which I couldn't help noticing were rather old and shabby.

"Well then why don't we organize a double exhibition for the two of them?" suggested Olga, her eyes lighting up in that stupid way she has.

"No, no, no!" my husband objected categorically, now behaving boorishly, even downright offensively, in a manner in which he'd normally never allow himself to act in front of his business associates. "The young one's a professional, you see, while the old one's just an amateur."

And he didn't stop there, either.

"My wife's art, if you can call it that . . . Ha, ha, ha!" he blundered on, laughing to himself loudly. "My wife's art is more—how can I put it? It's more likely to appeal to the masses. That's why it's good for humanitarian purposes, you see."

"Did I tell you how *wonderful* you look?" said Olga, suddenly turning to face me. But I was glaring at my husband and the words had already flown out of my mouth.

"Don't you *ever, ever* talk about my art that way again!" I yelled. "Is that understood?" As if from a distance, I could hear my own voice, sharp and high-pitched, I could see myself repeatedly jabbing my index finger at my husband's chest.

"Okay, okay, I'm sorry!" he said, holding up his arms as if in surrender and stepping backward away from me, still grasping his glass of vodka between thumb and one finger. He was about to take another step backward when he tripped and fell heavily on his ass.

After which there are some gaps in my memory of that night.

The next day was a Sunday and I woke up late, with a pounding headache. My temples throbbed. Everything was eerily quiet, though it was clear and sunny outside. The bright light was making my headache even worse, so I closed all the shutters and lay down again, closing my eyes. Gradually I became aware of all the sounds around me: a dull buzzing in my ears, then the rustling of leaves outside, the creaking of the roof, the hum of a distant car. And then, a little later, two people speaking in hushed voices.

I got out of bed and tiptoed up the stairs, following the sound of the conversation. It grew clearer and clearer as I got closer to my husband's study. From behind the door I could now hear clearly the hushed voices of my husband and my niece. I pressed my ear against the door and closed my eyes:

"But if I did apologize to her, it wouldn't be sincere," he was saying.

"You really should say you're sorry, though," my niece said. "You shouldn't have spoken your thoughts out loud. Not in public . . ."

"I can't do it! Maybe she finally needs to realize her paintings are like the daubs of a third-grader. She makes me embarrassed in front of my colleagues! And now I've gone and organized an exhibition for her. I'll die of shame if it actually happens!"

They were both silent for a moment.

"Maybe you could give her a few lessons?" he said at last, "I mean teach her a few things."

"It's hopeless," replied my niece. "She's got no talent whatsoever, but at the same time she's extremely vain. I once tried to explain a few things to her and, well . . . I can't even begin to describe the look she gave me, the rage in her eyes! It frightened me. She can get really violent."

"Tell me about it. You saw how she acted last night."

"I'm scared she'll kick me out."

"She can't kick you out. This is my house."

"It's hers too."

"True . . . But still, she does like you. And I like you a lot. I don't know what to do. I've tried so many times to persuade her to seek help for her drinking. I even found her a really good shrink, the wife of one of my colleagues. But she just accused me of trying to make out she was crazy and that's as far as it went. Then she told me that I was the drunk and that I was projecting my problems onto her because I couldn't face the fact that it was me who was the alcoholic."

"Okay, but let's be honest: you both drink. I do, as well."

"That's true," he said, "but she drinks to escape from her pain, whereas we drink because we're happy. Oh God, I just don't know what to do!"

"Maybe she'll get over it? Maybe it's just that she still hasn't worked out what to do with herself now that her kids have left home?"

"That's exactly it," he said. "Empty-nest syndrome."

"Yup. Empty-nest syndrome."

It was then that the throbbing pain in my head moved to the pit of my stomach. Every breath came painfully. My legs were so heavy I could barely make it down the stairs. Inside my studio I stood in front of the easel and grabbed a brush. I wanted to paint the blackness inside me and the leaden weight in my thighs and knees. But I just stood there and stood there and stood there in front of the blank canvas, not knowing what to do.

A Creature of Habit

IT'S UNCERTAIN HOW much longer my husband will remain an ambassador. He may be recalled or have to resign because of me. Of course, this is not something we talk about. When he comes home from work, he goes outside into the garden, settles into his deck chair, drinks a vodka on the rocks, and smokes a cigar. My Manoli drinks vodka too, but always straight, never with ice. No, wait, that's a lie. He'll add ice every once in a while, to give himself a change, saying: "Sometimes you've got to shake things up a bit." That thing about "shaking things up" ties in neatly with his whole philosophy of life. He likes change. Frequent change. Every few weeks, he rearranges his pictures or furniture. Nothing major. Unlike my mom, who used to do up the whole apartment every few years. Her shrink said it was brought on by her need to "escape herself," to "rediscover herself in a new environment" or something. With Manoli, the changes aren't so severe. His changes are small and sweet. He sticks to his habits. I, for one, would love to become a habit of his, a permanent fixture in his life, like that girl he was with before me. That young slut, Maya. I don't know how old the little slut was when she got her claws on him, but of all the crazy bitches in this world—I say good riddance. Thankfully, she found herself someone richer and more famous, and dumped my Manoli. Otherwise it's hard to say what he would have done. Maybe he would have stayed with her. Luckily, I came along. I want to be a long-term habit of his. I want him to possess me forever, even though I know he might occasionally want to change things, like he does with the furniture. But now it looks as if I might be leaving for a new posting with my ambassador husband. In a day or two, I think I'll try to talk to him and see if what others are calling a "scandal" can somehow be swept under the carpet, because I really want to stay here, where Manoli is and where I met him. If I leave, there's no doubt Manoli will start making changes. It's not as if he's not good looking and the women don't stick to him like glue. He really likes them a lot, too, especially when he's drunk. But let's not beat around the bush: he's drunk most of the time. You could never drag him away from that goddamn bar, although because of me he's stopped going there so often. Unless, that is, he decided to drink somewhere else and switched bars. That would never happen with my husband. It's ironic, I know, given that my husband and I are constantly on the move due to his postings, but he doesn't like change. Still, he frequently has to change the most important thing of all: his home. But really, he doesn't like to change a thing. A case in point: every day, after he comes home from work, he sits in the garden, drinks his vodka from the same glass and smokes the same cigars he's been smoking his whole life. The only thing new is that he's now also grieving the death of his dog: a fawn-colored Great Dane. I never liked the dog. It was too big. It didn't like me either, so I kept out of its way. Just imagine traveling with a dog that big. Of all the creatures in the world, my husband had to go and choose a Great Dane, probably hoping it would anchor him somehow. One of the advantages of his job is that, when he speaks in public or prepares for a formal occasion, he always behaves in the same way and says the same things. Mainly just empty words, things nobody wants to listen to, delivered time and again at receptions and events. But with Manoli, each of his performances is different. One play he starred in I saw nineteen times. Not to mention all the other plays in which he didn't have the lead role. At first, he was flattered. But after the tenth time, I could see he was starting to get a little worried. I know it's not normal, but I just couldn't help myself. Not only did I feel exhilarated when I saw him on stage, as if my soul was soaring aloft, but I shivered every time I remembered us making love. Plus I'd start to throb down there. This is not how I would express it to him. I would often say that he really turned me on, that I became engorged, as moist as a dewy spring bud, every time I saw or thought of him. But I didn't tell him how I felt when I was watching him on stage. I had a feeling he'd get worked up about it. Instead I told him I was studying his performance, that I was trying to work out how an actor creates a connection with the audience, and that every audience expects something new from a good actor. When I said this, Manoli smiled and asked if I was a theater critic. No, I said. He asked me what I did for a living; he'd never asked before. Luckily for me, since I don't have a job. My husband's the one with the job. To be honest, he's like an actor too. He constantly acts as if he's not bothered at all by the countries we're posted to. That he doesn't think the people who live here are uncivilized brutes always at each other's throats. Whenever the embassy sponsors an organization, he acts as if he cares, especially if it has anything to do with the arts and culture. He goes to receptions, official openings, and other events, where he gives the same speeches holding a glass of white wine raised high, wearing the same smile and the same pin on his lapel with the Macedonian flag and our own country's flag lovingly entwined. I usually down two whiskeys before we leave for a reception. This is how I'm able to be more relaxed and sociable with the locals. I know I must come across as strange, with my face all flushed like that. But Manoli says my eyes sparkle and become glassy. Your beautiful eyes, he always used to say when we first met. My husband used to say that to me too, that he fell in love with me because of my eyes. But he hasn't mentioned my eyes in years. Or kissed them. Whereas Manoli kissed them a lot. Before he moved on to someone else, that is. You're gorgeous, you look great for your age, he'd say to me. Wow, you're stunning. You're rocking that dress. You look hot in your heels. Sometimes he'd want to make love while I was wearing a hat from a function that I'd been to—or rather a function that *we'd* been to, since, being a celebrity, he'd often attend them too. There were a few times when I rushed over to his place after a function or event and he'd make me take all my clothes off except for the hat and heels. Then he'd take me from behind. My husband—he doesn't do that anymore. If we make love at all, he insists I be on top. But he no longer turns me on. There's his bald, pointy head, his thin lips, his gray stubble when he can't be bothered to shave over the weekend. His liver spots. His scrawny arms and legs. And with all that, I'm expected to get on top and ride him. Meaning, it's me who has to do all the work. It would be easier if I were the one lying down. There are times with Manoli when I'm lying down, but mainly he likes to take me from behind, except when he's blind drunk—then he wants me on top. Unlike Manoli, my husband just has the one vodka when he comes home from work, and smokes the one cigar. He sticks to that one glass of vodka even now that the dog he loved so much is dead. I thought maybe with the death of the dog and the likelihood that he'd have to resign, he might start drinking a bit more, or just want to talk to me, but as I said, he's a creature of habit, someone who doesn't like change, someone who pretends things haven't changed. Then there's Manoli, who, as I've already said, likes change. And that's what made things different between us. First, I saw him with a girl after one of his plays, another little slut, like Maya, his ex. You should have seen her drooling all over him. She was like a stocky little mushroom compared to Manoli, who's very tall. I went up to him, grabbed his arm, and dragged him outside. Then I started going to the bar where he drank at night after the plays he was in, and even after those he hadn't been in. Some of those slutty actresses, whom he's probably fucked in the past and is probably fucking still —just for the sake of variety—go to that bar too. I've sat at their table a few times and made everyone speak English because, of course, I don't speak Macedonian. I'm no fool, I know that kills the conversation. One by one, they all disappear and he ends up all mine. I used to do that a lot: go to the bar at night, pick him up before he had more drinks than he could handle, take him back to his place, and have him make love to me in my heels, for a whole hour, if that's what it took. But those little whores started getting more and more on my nerves, especially those young student actresses. One night I caught him red-handed. They were sitting at a table in the bar. He was nibbling her ear, she was cackling. I went up to them and slapped her face. I told him to get up and leave with me immediately. He hugged the girl, who was crying because I hit her hard, something she deserved. He yelled, "You're crazy, leave me alone!" Things like that. Of course, he didn't mean it, but he had to act as if he did because I really did belt that girl; he had to defend her. Looking back on it now, that was a bad move on my part. I told him I wouldn't leave unless he came with me. He went on yelling at me. I don't know what came over me, but I screamed. He disappeared somewhere behind the bar. I tried to go after him, but the owner of the bar stopped me. I'm pretty sure I broke a few bottles that were on the counter and tried to smash a wine glass over the girl's head. But I ended up smashing it over the head of some other woman sitting behind her. I feel bad about hitting that other woman. I felt two pairs of arms grab me then haul me outside. I tried to break free. Then a car from the embassy pulled up. I was shoved inside and driven home, where my husband was waiting for me. He was pale but calm. All he said was that I should take a bath and calm down. He told me we probably wouldn't be staying in Macedonia any longer. Then he went out into the garden and, can you imagine? he lit a cigarette, doing something different for once. As for what I think about the whole situation, I'm sure Manoli doesn't want anyone to replace me. He just wants to change the dynamics in our relationship. Whereas my husband—he'll never change a thing. He didn't light up another cigarette. So we may just end up staying here.

Father

I GAVE BIRTH to our son in September. He was a week late, but even when it was time, he didn't want to come out. It took me a while to come around after the delivery. I don't remember how long exactly. All I know is that when they brought him to me, I felt nothing but fatigue and anxiety, and later on some other, rather unpleasant, feelings. I thought it must be a sign. A sign that things between us would not be the best, the way they're meant to be between mother and son.

They put him in my arms and I looked at him. He was swaddled like a cabbage roll. His face was scrunched up and reddish-purple, like an elderly man gasping for breath. His eyes were watery, vacant. There was nothing in his eyes except the fluid that had nourished him for nine months. His mouth moved, but there was no sound other than his lips smacking. "Lay him on your breast," said the nurse. I did so. For the first time, I felt him pulling at me, sucking on me. And until I pulled him off, the whole time he did that, I felt as if I was being milked by a small alien.

That same night my husband threw a party at our place. As is the custom, he invited all our friends and relatives over for pancakes. About fifty people traipsed through our apartment and used my bathroom to take a piss or even a shit. Some of them probably fished around in the medicine cabinet, rummaged through my makeup and perfumes, peeked at my sanitary pads and expired tampons. They littered the new carpet with cheese

83

crumbs. They trampled over the crumbs and crammed them deep into the fibers. My cousin Zharko will have been lurking in front of the bathroom door, ready to pounce on any woman who emerged, trying to impress her with his total lack of humor. My husband will have been playing the guitar, raising his glass between every song, spilling rakija all over the place. "Your first-born's a boy!" they all cried out, and: "Congratulations, well done champ."

While all this was going on, I lay alone and weak in a hospital bed, trying to get some sleep. But they kept putting my newborn son in my arms. From that first day he cried a lot and wanted to feed all the time. His most developed features were his senses of smell and taste, and he had just one instinct: to swallow greed-ily. He'd screw up his nose before I put him to my breast. Then he'd pucker his lips and make sucking sounds until he clamped his mouth on my nipple. He did that when we brought him home too. He'd wake every hour, wanting to feed. When he fin-ished, I'd put him down in his crib and rock him. The moment I stopped rocking him, he'd start to scream. So I'd just let him scream. I'd read on online mothers' message boards that this was one kind of sleep training method: leave the baby to scream and cry so it gets the message that nobody's coming to pick it up and rock it. In the end the baby falls asleep on its own. And that's what I did. I'd go to bed, while he screamed in the next room. At first, my husband didn't wake up when our son cried. But not long after that, the crying woke him up too. He'd open one eye and watch me leave the room. Soon I stopped getting up right away when I heard the baby crying. My husband would pick him up and bring him into the bedroom. "You stay in bed, sweetie. I'll bring him to you," he'd say to me and then he'd come back, tou-sled and half asleep, with the baby in his arms, and gently place him on my breast. "Come on, stop crying now," he'd say quietly and gently, caressing the baby's cheeks and mine.

I followed the sleep training method and left the baby to scream in the other room after putting him down to sleep, but my husband couldn't take it and went to sleep in the room with him. After a while, I stopped hearing him at all.

"Motherhood is divine," other mothers, all of them my friends, said to me. "If I'd known it was like this, I would have become a mother long ago. I don't know why I waited so long," they would tell each other. "There's no better feeling than when it's feeding from you," they would say, smiling sublimely at one another. "The moment my child was born, I felt it was a part of me," they would sigh happily. I, on the other hand, felt a rising panic. "I'd like to have one more, but I don't know if we'll have time. Ana, why don't you have another, while Luca's still young? He'll have a little brother or sister to play with then. Plus you have such a wonderful husband. You should see mine . . . he doesn't lift a finger at home. That's why having a second one is out of the question for me."

It's true that my husband never lets go of Luca. I spent the time mostly lying on the couch, watching TV. When Luca stopped waking up in the night, I started sleeping a lot more. Occasionally I'd have to feed him, but soon even that came to an end.

"Look at how sweet he is," my husband kept telling me. He'd bring him to me while I was lying down and place him in my lap. "He's so sweet," he'd say to me. Luca was a fat baby, as solid as a cannon ball, probably because of all the milk he sucked out of me. And even though I didn't hold him much, my arms became big and muscular, almost like a bodybuilder's. After he'd finish feeding, I'd try to hold him for a bit, rock him on my knee, smile and laugh at him the way my husband did. Luca would kick and laugh and wave his hands, even though I wasn't doing anything special. "Look how much he likes you," my husband would say every time Luca played in my lap. I knew why he said it. It still didn't help.

My husband rarely loses his cool; he's very even-tempered. As my friends would say, he gives me "huge support" and I'm "a very lucky woman." He's only ever lost it in front of me once. We were looking at photos of Luca. My husband had taken a photo of him dressed in a baby romper, which was so tight on him that the bottom button had to be left undone. "Look how chubby he is," said my husband, laughing happily. In that photo Luca looks grotesque. He's smiling with his mouth wide open, showing his two gapped front teeth and his tongue is sticking out. His nose is wide and his nostrils are flared, gaping like the entrances to two little caves. His eyes are half closed, his eyebrows raised like the Joker's. He's clapping his hands with joy.

"He looks like a hippopotamus," I told my husband. He just gulped and changed the photo. I was in the next one. I was holding Luca.

"And you . . . you look like . . ." my husband's voice faltered then died away. "Do you have to hold him at arm's length in every single photo?" He flicked through the photos. In all of them, I had the same frozen look on my face, holding Luca in front of me with outstretched arms, as if I was handing him over to someone. In all of them, there was poor little Luca, all smiles.

Even the other mothers agreed that things get worse when a baby starts to walk. When that happened, I lost more weight. I also started taking Diazepam to help keep myself calm, because the noise levels at our place became unbearable. When Luca took his first steps, that's when my husband started horsing around. He'd tap on all the tables as if he were a drummer. He'd tap with his fingers, with spoons, with a pen, with whatever came to hand. Luca would squeal with delight whenever my husband did that. He'd be feeding Luca and then he'd tap with the little plastic spoon. Luca would squeal. He'd open his mouth wide and my husband would stick a spoonful of food inside. And they'd both scream with joy. My husband was so thrilled with Luca's screaming that he tapped even when Luca wasn't at home. He'd sit down at his desk and the tapping would begin right away. Each tap was like a direct blow to the back of my head.

My husband would also try to coax Luca to walk toward him by tapping. He'd sit cross-legged at one end of the room. He'd grab one of Luca's toys—a truck or a bulldozer. He'd take two markers and tap on the truck. First, Luca would squeal with delight. He'd climb unsteadily to his feet, which were so fat and clumsy that he looked like he'd never walk at all. Then he'd slowly toddle toward my husband. As he neared him, he'd let out a loud scream. He'd hang on to the couch and the coffee table for support, grabbing whatever object came to hand. Then he'd throw it on the floor. He destroyed everything in his path. Even just a simple turn to the left or the right would bring something crashing to the floor. My husband would laugh and Luca would squeal. I'd clean up the mess after they'd gone to bed. Every time I bent down to lift something off the floor, my head slowly throbbed.

Soon the headaches became more frequent and more painful. That happened when my husband taught Luca to run around the apartment. My husband worked from home and was never one for going out much anyway. He had asthma and a mild dose of agoraphobia. It was late January when Luca started toddling around. The air outside was thick with smog. On the news they warned parents not take their children outside. The same went for people with asthma. So my husband stopped taking Luca out at all. Like a puppy, Luca had nowhere to run around. That's why there was the ritual of chasing and running around the living room four times a day: when he got up in the morning, around midday, at six in the afternoon, and at nine-thirty in the evening, before he went to bed. My husband would chase him around the living room and Luca would scream with delight, toddling along on his wobbly legs, his body wiggling left and right like the hand of a metronome. Thump-thump-thump-thump-thump-thump-thump on the wooden floor—his steps echoed through the apartment and in my head like small hammer blows.

When my husband wasn't at home and Luca and I were alone, he'd run up and down like a caged monkey, making the same sounds he did when he ran around with my husband, even though I wasn't chasing him: excited guttural roars. When we were alone, he would yell out something that sounded like "a-ga, a-ga"—as if he were playing a game. The whole apartment shook, as if there was a baby elephant stomping around inside. I felt an explosive pain in my head. "He has to run around," my husband would say, as if Luca were a dog. "Otherwise he'll have problems sleeping. Look at him: he's full of beans and as healthy as an ox! He's like a little Hercules!" he'd chortle, his eyes shining with joy.

One day my husband was out and Luca was running around

alone in the living room before I put him to bed. I was sitting in the bathroom with the tap running. The sound of water flowing into a bucket drowned out the noise he was making. When the bucket was full, I went into the living room and found him sitting on the floor, hitting a toy truck with a wooden spoon. The doorbell rang and Luca looked at me. His cheeks were red and a string of snot was dripping from his nose.

A woman with glasses and an explosion of tight orange curls was standing at the door.

"Good evening, I'm the neighbor who lives below you," she said without giving me the opportunity to reply. "You've probably never seen me before, right?" she asked. I nodded. I didn't think there was anybody living below us. There had never been any sounds and I'd never seen anyone come out of the apartment below us, and certainly not someone with hair like that.

"That's because I rarely go out. But I'm here now because for quite some time I've tried to be understanding, since you have a small child. But I can't stand it anymore. You're extremely noisy and I'd appreciate it if you could stop running around the apartment. I can hear absolutely everything. The noise is so loud it even shakes the vases on my shelves. It's really unbearable. I'd like to ask you to be quieter if you could," she said all in one breath.

I nodded.

"I'm sorry," I muttered. "We'll be quieter."

"Thank you. You know, you really are noisy, otherwise I wouldn't have come over to complain. You've been noisy for a whole year now, and I've put up with it that long," she went on in a monotonous tone.

"Again, I'm sorry. You should have said something sooner. We didn't know there was anyone in the apartment below us."

"Yes, but I've tried to be understanding, you know . . . and I have been understanding!" she cried all of a sudden.

"Yes, of course. I'm sorry," I said again and took a step back.

But she didn't make a move. It was as if she had somehow gotten bigger and was towering over me, even though I knew she was standing in the same spot. Her lips curled, as if she were about to cry.

"Forgive me," she said in a strangled voice, "but I'm an academic and I need to concentrate. I'm almost always at home, because I work from home. I write books. I'm a researcher. I need peace and quiet." She paused and swallowed. Then she spoke a bit louder. "That's why I moved to this neighborhood. But I can't stand it anymore. You really must do something about it. Not only is there constant banging and screaming from your apartment," her small orange curls shook with every word she spoke, "but lately there's been running and stomping too. But tell me, miss, who chases their child around the house, as if the child were a dog? Can't you go outside? Even dogs are taken out for a run! Isn't there a big playground just down the road? Couldn't you just let your child run around in front of the apartment building? Why do you have to do it at home? Do you think that your child is happy?" her voice was becoming more and more high-pitched, louder and louder. She sprayed me with specks of saliva. Her loud voice echoed around the entrance hall. I felt as if I were stuck inside a seashell. It was as if I were about to black out. I heard a rumbling sound in my ears and my head ached like someone was ramming a screwdriver through my ear.

"You can't let a child run around at home!" she continued, now having lost all control. "A child needs to be outdoors! What you're doing is not only inconsiderate to me and detrimental to my work, but it's not fair on him either! Four times a day I have to put up with this earthquake in my own home, while the rest of the time I have to put up with small aftershocks, banging, and screaming. But, miss, all this running and stomping around and causing four earthquakes a day—I won't stand for it anymore!"

Right then, Luca ran over to me. Like a runaway car, he slammed into my leg and held onto my knee. "Uh?" he cried, the way he always does when he sees someone new. He smiled and looked at the neighbor. Her eyes bulged.

I shook him off and gave him a slap. Then another. Luca stayed silent, looking at me, and a small trickle of blood dripped from his nose. I looked at the neighbor. Her face grew long and pale, as if it were no longer hers. For a moment, there was deep silence and my head stopped hurting.

Saturday, Five in the Afternoon

MY HUSBAND IS a true gentleman. A rarity these days. When he steps inside a building, not only does he hold the door open for the lady, but the way he stands aside and waits for her to enter is simply dignified: with his head bent slightly toward her and a respectful smile. He takes care never to let a lady light her own cigarette. He never swears or talks loudly in front of ladies. He engages them in polite conversation, never asking anything too intimate, always letting them know how important they are. Naturally, he always uses the "vous" form of address with them.

He looks like a true gentleman too. He always wears a suit: matching pants and jacket, a shirt and vest underneath. Everything has to be impeccably clean and ironed; that's my job. His nails are always perfectly manicured, his mustache neatly combed and trimmed. His breath is always fresh from the mints he carries with him in a small tin. He keeps his grandfather watch, which never loses time, in his vest pocket, and an ironed handkerchief in his pants pocket. He wears a hat too, of course. And if he thinks it might rain, he carries a long black umbrella with a wooden handle.

He's also a family man. When our two children were small, he read to them before bed, took them to violin and piano lessons, to the park at weekends, the beach in summer. Now they're grown up, he sends them money in an envelope every month. After every home-cooked meal, he kisses my cheek and thanks me. He never raises his voice to me. Every year he buys me new pearl earrings. When we're out visiting or have guests over, he never interrupts me when I'm speaking. When we go out for a walk, he always takes my hand and we stroll leisurely hand in hand. I know everyone looks at us in admiration. Before we go to sleep, he kisses my lips and says "good night," always his final words of the day. Until recently, we used to make love twice a week: at night, with the lights turned off. He would never completely take off my long nightgown. Our lovemaking would last the same length of time. We would do the same thing.

But then two years ago we stopped making love. First it went down to once a week. Then to once a month. And then to never. My husband would still try to make love to me twice a week. He would do the same things he always did, but he simply couldn't penetrate me. He would then give me a kiss, go back to his side of the bed, and say "good night." Because he's a gentleman, he doesn't talk about things that are self-evident. So one night, he just said: "Velika, my darling. I'm fifteen years older than you."

One Saturday afternoon, exactly a year ago, he told me we were going to visit a friend, but he didn't say which friend. I didn't ask him because I had a feeling I shouldn't. We headed off along the lakeshore. People turned to stare at us because of how we look: we stroll leisurely along, our heads held high, smiling gently. We talked in low, steady voices. We reached our friend's house. "Isn't this Stojan's house?" I asked. He nodded and smiled, then rang the doorbell.

I've known Stojan since childhood. He wanted to be with me, but my parents and I decided that I would marry Petar instead. Later, Stojan and I would sometimes bump into each other in the *Charshiya*—the Old Bazaar—or sometimes at other people's dinner parties. His wife, Danica, died tragically—she drowned. Awful rumors spread about the accident, but I don't believe in those kinds of unsavory stories about alcohol and women. And so, he ended up a widower. Fortunately or not, they didn't have children.

Stojan invited us inside his house, which in no way compares with ours in terms of style and cleanliness. But I don't blame him. After all, he's a widower. As a widower, he had to make us coffee by himself. I wondered if it would be appropriate for me to offer to make it. I glanced at Petar, who gave me a blank look. So I just sat there with my hands folded in my lap. Stojan brought in the coffee, glasses of water, and little glass dishes of Turkish delight. He took out his pipe and started to smoke. He and Petar talked about work, about the local elections, about the level of pollution affecting the local lake. Every now and then, I would politely comment. As soon as he'd finished his coffee, Petar got up to go, but he put his hand on my shoulder and told me to stay. I looked at him in amazement, but his firm look suggested I shouldn't protest or ask questions; things would soon become clear. Petar has a sureness about him that always inspires trust in me, even when I get a nervous feeling in the pit of my stomach. "I'll be back in an hour," he said to me. It was five o'clock when he left. The doorbell rang on the dot of six. He took my hand and, once again, we strolled leisurely back home along the lakeshore. On warm afternoons there are even more people who jog along the lakeshore with little headphones in their ears. Everyone stares at us. Some of them openly smile. I admit, we may appear a little strange to them, but I think we're still likeable.

For the past year, at five o'clock every Saturday afternoon, Petar has dropped me off at Stojan's place and picked me up at six. Once, I asked him what he did during that hour. "I read the paper and sit on this bench," he said, pointing at the bench by the lake. "When it's raining, I sit at that table in that café over there. I read the paper and drink coffee," he said, pointing at a café not far from the lake.

Stojan and I sit in the living room and drink coffee. But it's me who makes the coffee now. I serve it on a tray together with the Turkish delight and a glass of water. After that he smokes his pipe while I slowly sip my coffee. We watch television together. He asks me what I want to watch. He has cable, so there are many choices. Often, I don't know what I want to watch, so he chooses, but it's always something to my liking. Petar won't allow us to have a television set or a computer at home. When our children come to visit after their exams, they bring some sort of phone with them. But Petar won't allow those contraptions in the house.

The children visit us much less often now because they go to graduate school.

At ten to six, I get up to wash the coffee cups and the small glass plates we use for the Turkish delight. Stojan stays on the couch, smoking his pipe and watching television. He has one of those new, thin flat screen types. When Petar rings, Stojan escorts me to the door. Then I leave with Petar.

On the way home, we talk about the elections, the weather, the polluted lake, what we're having for dinner the next day. Petar never asks me anything about my afternoons with Stojan. And I know he never will, like a true gentleman.

Lily

LILY WAS NOT a pretty child. I'd known that ever since she was born. She was quite a hairy baby, very dark. She was born with bushy hair, with eyebrows that almost met over her nose and that never thinned out. Her eyes were very small, but over time they began to gleam. She had long, delicate little fingers and toes, with curved and shiny nails that were never sharp, even when I cut them. Although he would have preferred a son, when Jovan saw Lily, his face lost all its sternness, became round and soft. His eyes misted over whenever he saw her. He'd take careful hold of her little fingers and toes, gently kiss them and nuzzle his face in them. *Liliana, Lily, Lilikins*, he'd coo while kissing her.

She was meant to be called Petra, after my mother, and if we'd had a boy, he'd have been named Risto after Jovan's father. But Jovan started calling her Lily, after his own mother, when he first laid eyes on her, and we never discussed the issue of her name any further. Lily stayed Lily, after his dead mother.

Jovan didn't like my mother at all. She reminded him of poverty and illness. After my father died, she lived alone in the village, poor and sick. She couldn't get out of bed. We sent money to my brother, and he and his wife went to see her and looked after her as much as they could. The rest of the time she just lay there all alone, with a sour smell clinging to her, the smell of a slow death. Every now and then a neighbor went over to help her. Jovan wouldn't let me go and look after her. That's why he regularly sent money for her instead. Before Lily was born, I'd wait until he was away on business and then I'd take the train to her place. I'd bake her some bread, cook her something, stroke the back of her bony hands, kiss her forehead, and take the last train back home at night. Whenever I showed up there, the neighbors looked daggers at me. They'd stare at me as if I were some kind of murderer. My brother stopped liking me as well, and his wife refused to have anything to do with me.

Jovan found out once that I'd left the house while I was pregnant. "Do you want to get sick?" he yelled, even though my mother wasn't suffering from anything contagious. "Do you want to kill my child?" he shouted, turning red with rage.

After Lily was born, not even once did I manage to take her to my mother's so she could see her. I waited for Lily to grow and start walking, so that we could sneak off to the village while Jovan was away on business. But Lily was a bit slow. She started walking late, and when she did start, she walked like a young fawn. She wasn't like the other children, with a strong, stomping gait. Her steps were tentative, fearful, and she was frail. Jovan felt like crying whenever he looked at her, and he would just carry her in his arms and kiss her. Then she'd laugh a little, although Lily didn't laugh much at all.

When we'd take her out for a walk in the stroller, the women in the neighborhood would stop to look at her, as they did with all the other little children. By the time of her first birthday, she didn't look like a girl at all. Her thick curly black hair was still short. She looked more like a boy. "May your little son live a long and healthy life," the neighborhood women would say. Jovan would get very angry. "She's a girl, her name's Lily," he corrected them. "Then put a hair clip on her so people will know she's a girl," one of the bolder women would shoot back.

By the time Lily was one and a half and had started walking more confidently, I decided to get her ears pierced. At first, I was afraid to tell Jovan. But when I did, he immediately approved because he felt slighted whenever people said Lily was a boy, and when they didn't say she was pretty. After getting her ears pierced, she cried for the rest of the day, her little earlobes red and swollen, and I cried with her. When Jovan came home, we were both exhausted from crying. Lily was hiccupping. I felt bad for hurting her and was afraid of what Jovan would say. But he just took her in his arms, planting kisses on her face and her fingers, and Lily calmed down.

A month later, I took out the earrings her ears had been pierced with and replaced them with the gold earrings my mother had given me when I last went to see her, back when I was pregnant. "Your belly is round like a ball, which means it's going to be a girl," she said to me, and gave me the gold earrings in the shape of flowers with red stones in the center. They were the earrings my mother had worn when she was young. I remember those earrings gently brushing against me when I hugged her and nuzzled her neck.

Jovan came home and saw Lily's earrings. He smiled. "They're really beautiful," he said. "Did you buy them?" They were quite old-fashioned. I would have had to lie about where I got them, but I wasn't sure I could pull it off. What if he asked where I bought them? "They're my grandmother's," I said. "Who gave them to you?" he asked. "My aunt gave them to me before she left for Australia," I lied. "They're very beautiful," he said once again. He touched Lily's earrings gently, and kissed her on the nose. I could hardly wait for Jovan to go away on business again. Then I could take Lily to my mother's so she could see her with the earrings.

It was September and we were making *ajvar*, the red pepper preserve we made every fall. I made it the way my mother had taught me. My sister-in-law's *ajvar* was never as good as mine or my mother's. I made it with my friend, Kristina. Jovan didn't know how much we made. He loved eating it. He said it was the best *ajvar* he'd ever tasted. When I told him it was my mother's recipe he didn't say a thing. He just kept eating.

Kristina and I were sitting in front of our apartment building, roasting and peeling peppers, stirring the *ajvar*, chatting. Lily was playing with Kristina's daughter on the lawn. Kristina's daughter was four years old. She treated Lily like a doll because Lily was slow and fragile, but Lily never cried or caused any trouble. Occasionally, we'd let them peel a pepper or we'd help them stir the mixture with the wooden spoon.

Kristina was a close friend and knew about the situation between Jovan and my mother. I told her I was making some extra ajvar and that I planned to take at least six jars to my mother, something Jovan didn't need to know. I also told her Jovan was going away on business the following week and that I planned to go to the village with Lily to see my mother. It would be the first time my mother had ever seen her, and Lily was going to wear my mother's earrings. My mother doesn't have long to live, I said to Kristina, watching the *ajvar* slowly bubbling.

We filled all the jars with *ajvar* when Jovan was at work so he wouldn't know how many there were for us, and how many would be left over for my mother. I put the six jars I'd set aside for her in a cardboard box, and the box inside a plastic bag. The bag was quite heavy. Not only did I have to carry Lily and the box, but also a diaper bag with all of Lily's things. I didn't take the stroller because it would have meant extra weight. I carried Lily in one arm, propped against my hip, and her bag and the box with the *ajvar* in the other.

We were the last passengers to board the train and I barely managed to find a compartment with a free seat. There was nowhere for me to put my belongings so a man helped me put the box and the bag with Lily's things in the rack above the seat. I sat Lily on my lap and we set off. Lily didn't cry, didn't complain. She played quietly with a toy, a little white lamb. When passengers inside the compartment thinned out a bit a few stations further on, I sat Lily on the seat next to me. Two elderly women were sitting opposite us. "What a sweet little girl," they commented. "Look at how quiet and well-mannered she is. *Ptu-ptu-ptu,*" they cooed, smiling at us. After that they started asking a lot of questions: where was my husband, did I work, where did we live, where was I going alone with the child. I didn't want to tell them anything because I was afraid they might be from our village or a neighboring one and word would get around that I'd come with Lily, and then Jovan might somehow find out we'd gone to see my mother. I didn't know how to avoid their questions, so I just kept silent, which came across as rude. Soon the old women began staring suspiciously at me, with their jaws clenched in protest, casting meaningful glances at one another. They got off at the station before ours without saying goodbye.

We were left alone in the compartment with a man who dozed the whole time and seemed rather unsociable. He was unshaven, unwashed, and stank of cheap salami. He was wearing a checked jacket, which was frayed at the sleeves and had a large grease stain on the collar. Under his jacket he wore a sweater that had small holes around the neckline and a larger one at his gut. His hands were rough, with black dirt under his nails and caked in the wrinkles on his fingers and palms. He opened one eye a couple of times and stared at us. When we arrived at our station, he left the compartment without offering to help me.

I got up to get the box of *ajvar* and the bag with Lily's things from the baggage rack above. I stood on tiptoes and tried to drag the bag with the box of *ajvar* down toward me. Just as I thought I had it in my hands, the train suddenly jerked forward, sending me sprawling backward. I fell to the ground and saw the bag with the *ajvar* fall on top of Lily's head and then land on the ground. The box inside the plastic bag broke open and I saw something red leak from it. Lily collapsed onto her side, slumped over the armrest of the seat.

Her eyes were closed and she was unconscious. I shook her and called out her name. I checked her head and saw that there was no blood anywhere. Then Lily slowly opened her little eyes. Her gaze was somewhat absent, unfocused. One eye seemed to be moving to the right while the other kept still. Her mouth suddenly crumpled and she whimpered softly. "Bam-Bam," she said, and grabbed her head. People passing through the carriage looked into the compartment, but no one stopped to help. I hugged Lily, lifted her into my arms, and grabbed the handles of the bag containing the box with the *ajvar*. It was very heavy and I realized that it would soon break. A red, oily liquid had gathered at the bottom of the bag from the broken jar.

I got off the train. Lily was whimpering. At times she would start crying louder, but then quickly quiet down, as if she didn't have the strength to cry. "Bam-Bam," she repeated, holding her head with her little hand. The bag was getting heavy in my left hand and I was leaving a trail of red oily spots. It was at least a fifteen-minute walk to my mother's house. As I was walking, the plastic bag broke. I saw that two of the jars had cracked. I left the jars, the box, and the broken bag on the side of the road. I put two jars of *ajvar* into the diaper bag slung over my shoulder, cradled the other two jars in one arm, and carried Lily in the other. It started to drizzle. My hands and feet were shaking, my back was stiff, and I was drenched in sweat. Several people passed me but I didn't say hello because it was as if I didn't see them.

We arrived at my mother's place. She was asleep with the television blaring. When we went inside the house, the sound smacked me in the face and I turned the volume down because Lily started to cry even louder. The house was dark inside and smelled moldy and sour. My mother was fast asleep, snoring lightly with her mouth open.

I sat down on the small wooden stool beside her and put Lily on my lap. I felt around Lily's head, gently pressing it to see whether it was sore, or if there was a bump, and if she was bleeding anywhere. But Lily didn't react. Her gaze was empty and it seemed to me as though one of her eyes was moving a bit to the right again. She whimpered and cried for a bit, then stopped. She would say, "Bam-Bam," then stop speaking. I thought about putting her to bed and placing an ice pack on her head, but then realized that my mother didn't have a freezer. And I didn't want to put Lily to bed in my mother's house, which smelled of death. All I wanted to do was leave and take Lily home. I just wanted to lie down beside her, wake up the following day, and kiss her on her little nose and her little mouth. I'll never lie to Jovan again, I said to myself, and I'll never go to visit my mother ever again.

I wished that my mother were dead so that none of this would have happened. I looked at her snoring steadily with her mouth open. From it spread a stale, rotten stench. I looked at her and hated her for being alive, for not dying, for making me cause Lily harm. I had brought Lily here because of her, to this place that reeked of death.

I left the jars on the table, put Lily on my hip, and went out. I ran all the way to the station to catch the first train back. On a shabby bench on the platform that smelled of urine, I held Lily tightly and stroked her head. She had stopped whimpering, and was calm and breathing evenly. But she wasn't the same Lily. I could sense that, even though I couldn't say why.

Instead of going straight home, I went to Kristina's. Her husband and her children were home. She was baking pita. She was covered in flour up to her ears. She took fright when she saw me. Goodness knows what I must have looked like. She pulled me and Lily into the kitchen and closed the door.

Once the door was closed, I burst into tears. I held Lily tightly, but she was limp and showed no interest in anything. She looked sad and lost. My crying didn't seem to upset her the way it did whenever I argued with Jovan at home. Now she just stared at me and let out a small whimper, so I cuddled her and she stopped. I told Kristina what had happened.

"You have to take her to the hospital," Kristina said, gently stroking Lily's short black curls.

"What do you mean take her to the hospital? Jovan can never find out about this."

Kristina kept silent. I was silent too.

"It's nothing," I tried to reassure myself. "She's probably just had a slight concussion. I'll put her to bed early."

"Lily, Lily!" Kristina called out to her. Lily raised her head and looked toward her.

"Fine, it doesn't look like it's anything serious. But she looks dazed. I don't know what to tell you. Maybe you should still take her to the hospital."

"What do I tell Jovan? No matter whether I was at home alone, or at your place, it would still end up being my fault that Lily got hurt. He'll kill me. He can never find out."

Again Kristina said nothing and we both sat silently.

"Don't worry. You only see the bad side to things. Come on, it'll pass, she's a kid. Children are forever falling over and getting hurt then jumping up again," she finally said to me, trying to summon a smile.

"Yes, she'll get over it. It's nothing. Isn't that right, Lily? Does anything hurt, darling?"

"Bam-Bam," Lily said again, and grabbed her head.

We went home and I thought it best to let Lily sleep and rest. I put her to bed and then lay down on my own bed, which was next to hers. Kristina had tried to calm me down when we were at her place, but it hadn't worked. I waited for Lily to doze off and when I heard her breathing steadily, I took a pill, then fell asleep.

I woke up around midnight. Jovan was standing over Lily's bed and he was kissing her. "My little ducky," he whispered, kissing her fingers. Lily flinched slightly, but didn't wake up. Then Jovan lay down beside me and fell asleep.

Jovan's screams woke me in the middle of the night. He was screaming like a banshee, holding Lily in his arms and shaking her, but Lily wasn't moving. I managed to call the ambulance somehow, although I felt as if I were in a dream and I couldn't dial the number properly. All three of us got into the ambulance and went to the hospital. It was daybreak when they told us Lily had died. The doctors started asking me questions. How was the child behaving the previous day? Had she fallen over or been hit by someone perhaps? I told them that everything was as usual, like every other day. I told them that Lily had hardly cried at all, nor had she behaved strangely. We'd been at home the entire day, and in the afternoon, we'd gone to visit my friend—Kristina, I said, and glanced at Jovan. She behaved normally there as well, I told them.

The doctor asked us if Lily had had any health problems, and whether there were any hereditary diseases in our family. I shook my head, while Jovan bit down on his clenched fist and squeezed his eyes tightly shut. "I had a brother who died of stroke when he was a baby," he said. I didn't know about that. The doctor simply nodded, and concluded that it was most probably due to this same cause.

Around midday I rang Kristina to tell her Lily had died. I told her the funeral would be held at noon the following day. And I told her Jovan knew nothing. If anyone asks, Lily and I came to visit you in the afternoon and Lily was her normal self. "Okay?" I asked. Kristina said nothing. I heard her sniffling on the other end of the phone. I hung up because I didn't want to hear her crying.

It was particularly painful for me to look at Kristina and Jovan at the funeral. But they were around me the entire time, howling with grief. Kristina just kept staring at me with a fixed gaze, her mouth half-open and wet with spit, emitting a vague moan. She didn't even try to use a handkerchief so we wouldn't all have to stare at her slobbering mouth. Jovan wasn't himself and looked awful. The whole time he held on to my sleeve, pulling me down. I could barely stand upright myself anyway, and I felt like just getting down on the ground and crawling. I didn't need his extra weight. At one point we both tumbled over and the mourners broke into a cry. Someone grabbed me from behind so roughly that it left two bruises on my arms. I tore my pantyhose and my feet got muddy because it had been raining all that day. Some stupid relative said the heavens were crying for Lily and then patted me on the back. A shiver of disgust ran down my spine.

After the funeral, Jovan changed dramatically overnight. His face sagged, his eyes became permanently teary. He went bald and gray. All that was left of his hair was a band around his scalp and a white tuft above his forehead. No longer a big solid man, he became small and meek. Even his demeanor softened, which disgusted me. He stopped going away on business trips so often, and began going to bed at the same time as me, which kept me from falling asleep. He'd lie down beside me and hug me. He'd start to snore as soon as he fell asleep, and after a while he'd stop snoring and toss and turn, whimper and groan. I'd wake him and he'd burrow even closer into me and hug me and stroke me. He'd whimper quietly and then fall back asleep. The first month I was too afraid to move or say a word. But I soon realized I didn't have to be afraid of him. I kicked him out of our bed. "Just don't make me sleep in a different room," he pleaded. So we slept in separate beds in the same room.

After a while I noticed his attitude toward my mother was softening. The first time he mentioned her, he said Lily had looked a bit like her. This observation seemed to me in poor taste as he was probably alluding to her eyebrows, which met above her nose. When Lily was alive, he always said she looked like his own mother. Now all of a sudden, according to him, Lily began to look like my mother. That also galled me, but I didn't say anything. After a few days he mentioned my mother again, while we were having lunch. I had cooked a vegetable and meat stew. Chewing away, he said I was the only person who could make such a delicious stew. Then he just swallowed and stared at me. His mouth was covered in grease because he never remembered to wipe his face with a napkin. "Your mother taught you to cook well. It's a pity she got sick." Again I said nothing. "How's your mother?" he asked, cutting another thick slice of bread. I shrugged. I didn't feel like talking about my mother. I hadn't been to see her since Lily died, and her life was just an added burden on me. "Have you heard from your brother?" he continued. "No," I lied. My mother was the same as she'd always been. Sick, poor, and immobile.

But Jovan wanted to keep on talking about her. One day he suddenly asked: "When are we going to your mother's?" No doubt I gave him a puzzled look because his teary eyes widened. He wanted to say something, but nothing came out. "I'll go alone," I said. But I didn't go. I didn't want to. I was sick of my mother and of him, and at times I wished them both dead.

But Jovan didn't let up asking when we'd be going to my mother's. "There's no reason for you to do that. You've never visited her before. She never saw Lily, and now you want us both to go. Stop making a mockery of her," I said.

He bowed his head so all I could see was the tuft of hair. He was like an old child. "Okay, just go alone," he said. He took some money out of his pocket and gave it to me. There was quite a bit.

"Don't go by train. Take a cab instead," he said. "We have the money."

I took the money and the following day, after he left for work, I put it in my pocket and went out. I didn't want to visit my mother. I headed toward the shopping mall downtown. At one store I bought myself some leather gloves, at another a silk scarf. I could easily hide them until I told Jovan I needed some money to buy a scarf and gloves. I put them in my bag. I could hardly wait to sit down somewhere so I could admire them, feel how soft they were, savor their smell of newness. Then I went to a restaurant. I sat down in a corner where no one could see me. I didn't feel like eating, but I didn't have anything to do, and I'd never been to a restaurant alone before. For starters I ordered a *pindjur* tomato and red pepper dish, with bread and cheese, even though I wasn't hungry. But when the food arrived, the bread was warm and the cheese was soft and the *pindjur* was refreshing. After I'd eaten, I felt better. Then I ordered a burger with a side of boiled vegetables. I also ordered a glass of red wine. Before the food arrived, I unpacked the gloves and the scarf and smelled them, rubbing them gently against my cheek. I felt good. I didn't feel like crying anymore. The food arrived and I ate all of it. I ordered baklava for dessert, and then some ice cream. I took out the gloves and the scarf once again and admired them. As I still had time, I went to the cinema. I didn't care what film I saw. It was some sort of historical film. I dozed off in the big theater seat and when the film finished, I went home.

"How's your mother?" Jovan asked me when he got home from work.

"The same as always," I said. Suddenly I burped up onions. I was worried the smell might give me away.

"What did you have to eat there?" he asked, as if he knew what I'd been doing.

"I made her some hamburger patties with onions. I bought some meat before I went to see her." I was surprised at how quickly I made something up.

"Mm, delicious," Jovan said, smiling. He then came over and gave me a big hug, while I just stood there like a pillar. "Go there again next week," he said to me.

"If you say so," I agreed.

*

My mother passed away six and a half months after Lily died. It was a relief to me, but Jovan was visibly shaken. He followed me around and stared at me all the time. He kept asking me if I needed anything, made me coffee, bought me sweets. The day after she died he even made dinner for us both. He paid for the funeral, the plot, and the gravestone, but I managed to persuade him that we needn't go to the funeral itself. I told my brother and my sister-in-law that we couldn't deal with another burial. They just sighed on the other end of the phone. Kristina also came over when she found out. Ever since Lily died, I'd been avoiding her.

We sat opposite one another in the kitchen, at the breakfast table. That was where I used to drink coffee with her and my other friends, before Lily died. She was staring at me, sniffling and nervously picking at the skin around her fingernails.

"How are you?"

"All right."

"You've put on some weight," she said.

I made no reply. I didn't care if I was fat or thin, and I didn't think it was any of her business. Then she started talking about my mother—what a lovely woman she'd been, what a hard life she'd had. She also said something stupid to try to comfort me, something along the lines of my mother having two children of whom she could be proud.

"What pride are you talking about, Kristina?" I couldn't help myself. "I left her lying sick at home and didn't go to see her for two years. When I went to see her with Lily, I didn't wake her up. She died without having seen her granddaughter. I didn't name my child after her."

"That's because of your circumstances," she said to me. "I'm sure she understood. Your father was a difficult man, too."

We sat there silently. She took my hand and squeezed it. Suddenly I burst into tears. She started crying too.

"You've got to tell Jovan," she said.

"Tell him what?"

"Well, you know," she said.

"That's the stupidest thing I've ever heard," I shot back. "Why should I tell him that? Do you want me to die too?"

"You'll die of a bad conscience. Secrets can eat at you from the inside," she said, and started crying again. "I have nightmares every night. I think if you don't tell him, something terrible will happen."

"What could be worse than what's already happened? Stop talking nonsense."

"It's not fair on him. Don't you see how he's changed? All he does is run after you. As if he thinks it's his fault."

"It *is* his fault," I said to Kristina.

*

When Jovan and I went to bed that night, before he fell asleep, I heard him sobbing. "What is it now?" I asked him.

"Forgive me."

"For what?"

"For your mother."

A silence fell between us.

"I was afraid of her illness. I thought something might happen either to you or to Lily if you went to visit her. The thought of her and her house and the village and everything frightened and disgusted me. I wanted to keep you away from all that."

I said nothing. He tried to steady his voice.

"But in the end Lily died because of me. Her illness came from my family. It's all my fault," he said, and burst out crying.

It's your fault, I wanted to say to him. *You're to blame, and no one else. It's your fault, your fault, your fault*, I kept saying to myself, while aloud I told him to stop talking nonsense, to let me get some sleep, and to stop giving me a hard time because it was *my* mother who'd died, not his.

*

That night I dreamed that Kristina and I were sitting out in front of our apartment building, stirring *ajvar*. The *ajvar* was thick and unnaturally red. We were laughing and chatting like we used to. I liked being with Kristina and I felt relaxed around her. But suddenly a hush came over the whole neighborhood. The quiet enveloped us. We fell silent and continued to stir the *ajvar* slowly. Our hands and nails were red from peeling peppers. It got harder and harder to stir the *ajvar* with the wooden spoon. I looked at Kristina. Her eyes were red and swollen. *I'm going to tell him*, she said. *I'm going to tell him*, she repeated. *You won't say anything*, I told her, and somehow, I knew my words would be hypnotic and she would do whatever I told her to do. All of a sudden, the spoon got stuck in the pot. I looked inside. *The* ajvar was glowing red and was as smooth as water. The spoon was caught on something. I could barely manage to lift it out. On the tip of the spoon were wet black curls. I put the spoon back into the pot and then pulled a black hair out of my mouth. Just as I drew it out, I felt another one in there, and I pulled a whole handful of curls out of my throat. I looked at Kristina worriedly, but instead of her, opposite me I saw my mother wearing Lily's earrings. She was stirring the *ajvar* and smiling at me, and her mouth smelled sour and reeked of decay. I opened my eyes and saw Jovan standing over me. His mouth smelled like my mother's and he was shaking me awake.

The Eighth of March

NONE OF THIS would have happened if we hadn't met Irena at the restaurant that night. That plus the fact I was totally under the influence of my academic supervisor, who for months had been telling me I should find a lover. "Why are you all dressed up? You look great! Did you finally find someone?" she'd say whenever we met for coffee, adding, "Every successful woman should have a lover!" which just confused me, because the conversation would then invariably turn to her husband, the weekend getaway he'd arranged at great expense or all the gifts he'd shower on her. She was so enamored, she'd often ring him up when we were together and bill and coo whenever she thought I wasn't listening.

But then she would go back to, "It's time you found yourself a lover. I can tell." She said it so often that I began to suspect that maybe she wasn't really happy in her marriage, but there wasn't a scrap of evidence to support my conjecture. Her insistence on my finding a lover got me thinking that something was wrong with me. I must look like someone who needs more sex, I thought to myself. Oh, and then there was the time we were having coffee when a well-dressed man with a thick head of graying hair stepped inside the café. "Sanya," my supervisor whispered, gripping my hand, "There's the guy for you!" He wasn't really my type, though I admit he wasn't bad looking.

"Okay, then why don't you tell me: how *do* I find a lover?" I finally asked. I made it sound like a joke, because whenever she said I needed a lover, she didn't sound entirely serious. I was dying to ask whether she herself had a lover, but I knew she wouldn't have told me. The boundaries between us were quite clear: she did the asking, I did the answering. But she did answer this question, at least: "When you really want something, anything is possible."

Frankly, I couldn't imagine having a lover. I'd never been unfaithful to Boban. I'd never even thought about having one. For I've never met a man who appeals to me half as much as Boban. I've always felt content with him. We've never argued and he treats me well. We're a happy family of four. These days, it's true, we rarely make love. Maybe once a month. But frankly, I don't feel the need to do it anymore. Boban and I have been together over twenty years, so maybe we're past all that now. But sometimes, when there's a love scene on TV with an actor I like—it's only actors that appeal to me, not real people—something stirs inside me. The last time this happened, I thought why not seize the moment? But I was embarrassed to say I'd been aroused by a scene in a film, so I decided to go about it more subtly. I turned toward Boban suggestively, but he was fast asleep on the couch.

So now I'm really pissed off at my supervisor for planting the idea in my head. If she thinks that I should have a lover—she's savvy, sure, and highly sophisticated—then maybe there really *is* something wrong with me. I'd heeded her advice my whole adult life and I'd rarely taken a wrong step. Until now.

But it wasn't just my supervisor's fault. It was that horrible creature, Irena, who deserves half the blame, showing up the way she did at the Three Pheasants Restaurant, where the director of our institute had invited us to celebrate the Eighth of March— International Women's Day. The restaurant was packed, a band were blaring folksy music, everyone was having a wonderful time, except Irena, of course. All our meals and drinks had been paid for in advance by our colleagues of the so-called stronger sex. Which is what set Irena off and made her make such a scene as she was leaving. "How chauvinistic can you get?" she blurted, slapping her money on the table to pay for all the rakija she had knocked back. "Can't you see that shit like this only reinforces our subjugation? On the one fucking day of the year they take notice of us, they buy us a few drinks, throw us a few flowers, and the rest of the year we're just their fucking slaves. But I guess that's what it means to be a Slav." "What rubbed you up the wrong way, Irena?" the men teased. "Didn't you get any flowers today? Or maybe it was something else you didn't get, huh?" Irena left in a huff. I was glad she'd left. I should have said something, too: "If you're such a perfect feminist, why did you bother coming to this party?" Maybe I'll save that for another day.

Strangely, when she showed up at the restaurant, she actually looked pretty good. She was all dressed up, which we'd never seen before. She usually shows up in jeans and sneakers, which I find perfectly unacceptable for a young professional, or any professional, for that matter. Frankly, if you ask me, no one should ever go to work in jeans, but who am I to say? I'd never seen her in a suit jacket, not to mention high heels. I doubt she's ever heard of a manicure, much less the idea of having her toenails done. And I'm thoroughly convinced she takes it as a point of honor to ignore her hair. She's got that naturally curly hair you can never straighten out. Nor does she wear makeup, though it would vastly improve her looks. As for jewelry, I hardly know where to begin: bits of woodchips she calls earrings and bracelets made of—I don't know, gravel or something. You couldn't pay me to wear that stuff. But the funny thing is, she could be quite attractive if she made the slightest effort. She has gorgeous legs, large breasts, and a cute little butt; no one would ever call her fat. And she's got that olive complexion, full lips, and green eyes that men swoon over. Or would, if she bothered to put some makeup on. A touch here, a touch there, and she could definitely turn a few heads, we all agreed, with a mixture of envy and regret.

I happened to be sitting next to Tony that evening. Tony's a slightly older colleague of mine. We went to the same high school and university, where he was once a teaching assistant, and now we work together. We get along pretty well on account of the fact that he too is married with children. When Irena showed up, we couldn't help following her with our eyes as she greeted the other colleagues. "Get a load of Irena," Tony said. "What's got into her?" he added, flashing me a cheeky grin. We chuckled. She was in a tight-fitting black dress that buttoned down the middle and showed off her curves. She wore emerald earrings that were shaped like tears, and green shoes and a green purse to match. She had clearly gone to some effort to spruce herself up. But the question was: Why? Wasn't she a die-hard feminist? Why would she stoop to conquer? She sat down next to me, but that was probably because it was one of the only empty seats in the place.

Tony had already drunk some rakija, and, like a gentleman, topped up my glass whenever I took a sip. He poured Irena a glass too.

"You look really nice, Irena," I told her.

"Thanks," she said, chewing her thumbnail. If she'd been wearing lipstick, she probably would have smudged it.

"Yeah, it's about time we got a real look at you. Ha, ha, ha," Tony said with a chuckle.

Irena continued chewing her thumbnail. "Thanks," she said, spitting out a bit of dead skin. How disgusting, I thought.

"Are you going out with your boyfriend later?" I asked, because I knew she'd been seeing someone for a while now.

"Yeah, we'll probably go out later," she said.

"Tsk, *boyfriend*," Tony said. "Are you still dating at your age?" Irena was about to reply, but Tony cut her off.

"How old are you now? Thirty-one, thirty-two? You've got your Masters and your PhD. So what're you waiting for?" Tony winked at her.

"Yes, why don't you two get married?" I asked her. I was genuinely interested to know. I couldn't understand why people did that: shack up together. I suspected one of them was waiting to see if someone better came along.

Irena just shrugged. "Why bother? We've been living together for years. It's like we're married."

"No, I'm sorry, excuse me," said Tony. "Marriage is marriage. A contract is a contract. Otherwise there's no trust."

"Come on, Irena, it's been ages since we've danced at someone's wedding," I threw in.

"No need for a big wedding, just buy us a drink and we'll

celebrate for you!" said Tony, raising his glass in a toast. The three of us clinked glasses, Irena reluctantly.

"You know what I really feel like eating?" said Tony all of a sudden, tapping his belly. His eyes gleamed from the rakija. "Pork liver."

"Oh, I'd love some too," I said, my mouth watering. "But there's garlic in it . . ."

"Let the singles worry about that," he said, grinning at Irena. An uncomfortable silence settled between us, because Irena didn't smile back.

He called the waiter over and ordered the liver, then resumed the conversation we were having.

"Okay, but seriously now, what's that boyfriend of yours waiting for? You'll miss the boat! If you wait much longer, you might not be able to get pregnant!" Tony said.

Irena opened her mouth to say something, but hesitated, so I cut her off, because all of a sudden—maybe it was the rakija—I felt overjoyed at being a mother and a professional. At being a stylish, elegant woman. I thought of Irena as my student, someone who needed my advice on life. Actually, I felt like my supervisor.

"The most important thing in the world is to have children, let me tell you. I had my first at twenty-seven, and now I regret not doing it sooner."

"Yeah. I'm sorry I only have one child. There's no greater gift in life than children," said Tony tenderly, looking at me.

"Nothing in life is more fulfilling than having a child," I insisted, inspired by the rakija. "A woman who's not a mother is an incomplete woman," I said, thinking of my unmarried aunt who suffers from hypochondria.

"Why don't you hassle some of the older colleagues instead of me?" Irena lashed out. The words tumbled clumsily from her mouth.

"There's no hope for them," said Tony. "They're thirty-six or thirty-seven and still unmarried. Do you really want to end up like that?" Tony seemed as concerned about her as I was. He had only been teasing her earlier, but now I realized that both Tony and I were doing this out of a sense of duty to a young colleague, a colleague with the potential to be both a beautiful and socially successful woman.

"End up like what?" asked Irena, with a frown that etched a sharp line between her brows. She suddenly looked a lot older. Tony lowered his voice and leaned closer to her. He glanced around to see if anyone else was listening, but they were all clapping their hands in unison with the violinist and the guitarist from the band, who had come down off the stage and were serenading two retirees from the institute. "Take Emma, for instance. Can't you see how frustrated she is because she's missed the chance to get married and have children?" Emma was always fighting with everybody, always trying to fix things, even to the point of going to war with people at the Ministry of Education. She looked like a lesbian. "Yeah," I nodded. "And the same goes for Nevenka, too." Nevenka was approaching forty.

"Doesn't Nevenka have a boyfriend?" Irena asked.

"She does," I said. "She's been with him for ages, if you're thinking of the same person I am. A big guy. A medico, I think. Not a bad catch, but, you know—he's 'secondhand goods.'" I imagined how awful it would be to be separated and reduced to going out with divorced fathers.

"Yeah, and afterwards things are just great for the man. He'll find some young chick to have by his side and take care of his own kid for him. You remember Mirjana?" Tony asked me. "She looked after her boyfriend's kid her whole life, and now she's forty-five and has no children of her own. She may have to adopt."

We both looked at Irena. She remained silent, nervously scratching the back of her head, as though tugging at something. How disgusting, I thought. She shouldn't do such things in public.

Just then, the liver arrived. Tony was delighted, and like a real gentleman, he scooped some onto my plate first, then, with a smile, attempted to serve some to Irena:

"So, we're agreed then. A wedding and a child a.s.a.p.," he said, winking at her and raising his fork, from which dangled a large chunk of liver.

Irena shoved his fork away and the meat landed on the tablecloth.

"What the fuck is it to you whether or not I have kids?" she erupted. Tony sat there with his fork still slightly raised. Irena spoke in a choking voice, through clenched teeth.

"I don't mess with your genitals, do I? So do me a favor and stay the fuck out of my twat."

What she said was so vulgar that we were both too shocked to reply. I'd never heard such words in public before. Especially from a woman.

"Look at the two of you! You sit there in your stinking, boring marriages and you want to drag everyone else down into your misery. You talk dirt about people's private lives and lecture others on morality and having a family, while you're probably screwing each other behind everyone's backs. You think I don't see the hanky-panky going on between you two? Give me a break!" Irena said, getting up from the table. She went and sat down next to the retirees, where she was soon to make the scene I described earlier and leave the party.

"What was that all about?" said Tony after Irena's rant.

"Young people nowadays. They have no respect for authority," I said, echoing the words my supervisor often repeated. My hands were shaking. Not just because of Irena's vulgarity. It was as if she'd said something about me I hadn't known, something intimate I hadn't been aware of.

"Incredible," said Tony, taking a bite of his pork liver. "Mm, this tastes good," he said, chomping away, breathing heavily through his nose, the frown on his face turning to a smile. Then, having regained his composure, he returned to the topic.

"Her behavior was unacceptable and can't be dismissed or taken lightly."

"Yes, there have to be repercussions," I said, wondering what I meant by that.

"You're right, we shouldn't work with her anymore."

"Well, you and I haven't worked together on a project in a long time." As soon as these words came flying out, I wondered why I'd said them. Something in Irena's rant had stung me, plus,

I was a little dazed from the rakija. Not knowing what else to do, I tasted the liver. It was delicious.

We talked about Irena some more, quickly finishing off the liver. Tony was constantly plying me with rakija. While we tried to have a serious conversation about a future project we could work on and recalled our first project together more than ten years ago, his face began to look more and more handsome to me. I wondered if I had similarly improved in his eyes. I realized I wasn't slouching anymore and adjusted my hair every time he looked at me.

"Tony's cute,'" my supervisor had once told me. "There's something special about his face . . . Something positively Neanderthal. Still, he's not bad for a caveman. He has a funny-looking body though. Have you noticed how skinny his little legs are?"

I was looking at the "Neanderthal" in Tony's face and realized his jutting brow actually appealed to me. His eyebrows were thick and dark, casting his eyes into shadow, eyes that sparkled like shiny sapphires. Every time he looked at me, I felt his eyes boring into me.

I thought about his "skinny little legs," too. Tony was tall, and yes, somewhat oddly built, but you could tell that as a young man he'd been attractive, before he developed the flab around his waist that made him pear-shaped. A bulge at the base of his neck gave the impression of a hunched back, and consequently a slight lack of self-confidence. His legs were long and spindly—feminine you might say—which is why my supervisor referred to them the way she did. But he had strong arms and huge hands with hair just below the knuckles. The gold band on his ring finger glinted in the light. I stared at it. Despite the glitter of scattered cutlery, the blaring folk music, the noisy, drunken revelers, and the ring of chubby women dancing around us, the wedding band glared at me.

"Sorry," Tony leaned in close to my ear, his lips brushing my hair. "My wife's calling me again. I'll have to answer."

"Hello!" he shouted into his cellphone, covering his mouth with the hand displaying his shiny wedding band. "I'm in a restaurant! What do you want?" he shouted. "No, I don't know when I'm coming home!" He hung up and made a point of slamming his phone down on the table.

He leaned closer toward me again. I felt his warm breath on my ear. The hairs on the back of my neck tingled. "Sorry," he said, "I really don't know what to do about her. She's such a pain in the ass." He pulled away from me, taking a big shot of rakija and giving me a helpless look.

"What, does she call you a lot when you're out?" I drew close, so close his cologne was rather overpowering.

"*All* the time," he said, rolling his eyes and gritting his clenched teeth. I noticed they were fake because they merged with his gums unnaturally. He leaned toward me again.

"You know, it's just that she doesn't know what to do with herself. She's obsessed with the house. Every day, all she does is clean the house and worry about what my daughter and I are going to eat. She thinks I'm reckless, that I go out too often, spend too much money buying everybody drinks. She complains I never help around the house, that I make her life hell. Sometimes she even calls me a drunk. Imagine that!" He said with a grin, clinking my glass. We took a gulp of our rakijas.

"So how much do you drink?" I ventured to ask.

"Nothing to get riled about, a drink or two once or twice a week. You know, with friends. In places like this. But every time I do, she gives me the same old crap: *When are you going to be back? What were you drinking? How much did you spend?*" he curled his lips and put on a falsetto voice to mimic his wife. Then he pulled away again, snapped his fingers and thumb together repeatedly to suggest someone babbling. "Blah, blah, blah!" he shouted. "She calls me all the time and screws everything up!" his shouting got louder.

I gently touched his arm. "Don't get all worked up," I said. "She's only being possessive. Just don't forget that you're an exceptional man," I blurted.

Leaning with one elbow on the table, he looked intently at me, his eyes a little unfocused. He was clearly dying to hear more.

"Don't forget that you're an outstanding intellectual. Besides which, you're a responsible husband and a wonderful father," I said, not knowing whether that was true. "Any woman would be lucky to be with you," I caught myself saying. The blood rushed to my face.

"Okay, well now you're taking it too far," he said, puffing up. He pulled his chair up to me. His chest swelled. His face lit up. "'Outstanding intellectual'—me?"

"You?" I said, as if astonished. "Well, you're one of the most respected experts in your field. A person with such detailed knowledge is rare," I repeated what my supervisor had once said about him.

"Oh, come on, now you *are* exaggerating," he said, his eyes crinkling with pleasure as he reached into his jacket pocket for his cigarettes.

"You think I'm only saying this because I'm married to some dumb cop?" That wasn't the first time I'd used that line to get a laugh. People said I was funny.

"You're witty," he said. "That's rare in a woman." I felt something rise in my chest. Pride, I thought to myself.

"Let's go outside and have a smoke. It's getting so noisy and crowded in here, I can barely hear you."

"Oh, I'd love a cigarette," I said, feeling an urge I hadn't felt in years. The last time I'd smoked was before I'd had my daughter, on a holiday in Herceg Novi, with Boban. That's when I got pregnant with her.

We went outside and stood under the eaves in the farthest end of the restaurant yard, where there was a wooden bench. Loud singing and an accordion solo blared from inside. We sat down on the bench and our hips touched. He handed me a cigarette and lit it for me with one of those lighters that have a huge flame and smell like a gas pump. He expertly flicked the lighter open and closed, the way I can do with a fan. My fingers trembled slightly as he lit my cigarette. I felt as though I were on a date, something I hadn't done in years.

"So it's like I was saying," he said, trying to resume our

conversation. I wanted to keep talking about personal things too. "Still, it's not easy."

"Everyone has problems. That's normal." I took a drag on the cigarette and felt nauseous, though I tried not to show it. I decided not to inhale so deeply next time. He remained silent and smoked, holding the cigarette between his thumb and forefinger.

"So, how *is* the cop?" he asked, with a playful grin. "Does he play the cop at home?"

"No, he's . . . he's . . ." I said. Surprised by the question, I took another deep drag on the cigarette and once again felt nauseous.

"He likes to go out too. But I never hassle him or ask him where he's been. He often works late and then goes out with his friends. Who knows where he goes and what he does?" I looked down at my high-heeled shoes. My slender feet looked terrific inside them. They gave me the courage to talk about things I probably shouldn't have discussed. I might even have exaggerated things a bit.

"Honestly, it doesn't bother me. Once the kids grew up, I finally realized what it means to have some peace and quiet. He goes out at night and I watch TV shows. Sometimes I watch them for hours. They help me unwind. I like those moments of solitude. Solitude is a luxury," I said, repeating another one of my supervisor's favorite lines.

"I shouldn't be saying this, but *I* would never leave you at home all alone," said Tony, taking a drag on his cigarette. I heard the sizzle of tobacco and then the sound of his breath as he exhaled the smoke. "Women like you are rare."

"Oh, come on now," I said, for it was clearly my turn to play coy.

"No, honestly," he turned to look at me, a thoughtful, faraway expression in his eyes. That was when the music in the restaurant stopped. Loud applause and cheers ensued.

"It looks like it's closing time," I said. "Ugh, now we have to go back inside and say goodbye to everyone," I sighed.

"Let's make a quick exit. Did you bring your car?"

"No, my husband has it tonight."

"Then I'll drive you home."

I knew he was a little drunk, but something told me to keep quiet and just let him drive. We headed over to the parking lot. We walked in silence, side by side, listening to the sound of our footsteps. I was sorry we were leaving. I didn't want the night to end and I wanted Tony to touch me. I longed for him to take me in his arms and kiss me, and felt no shame in wanting this. When we got into the car, the feeling grew even stronger, because this was now our place of intimacy, our temporary home. The smell of his cologne and the scent of lavender air freshener mingled in the air. He turned the key in the ignition and the engine purred into life. The dashboard lights lit up his face like the embers in a fireplace. The radio came on. By sheer coincidence, Vlado Janevski was singing: *You'll light up beside me like a firefly in the dark* . . . I felt woozy. I didn't ever want to leave the car. I didn't want us to drive off. I wanted it all to last forever. Just then his cell phone rang. His wife.

"Like hell am I going to answer that," he said, switching off the phone. "My battery's dead. Get it?" he said, shifting gears as he pulled out onto the main road. He looked so masculine to me at that moment.

Tony seemed lost in thought as he drove. I stole a glance at him now and then. Occasionally he took a sharp breath as if about to say something, but then let it go. Finally he mentioned how bright the Millennium Cross on Mount Vodno was that night. "Yes, it's beautiful," I half murmured, unsure whether I should admit I actually liked it. A few of the people at the institute hated the cross and admitting you liked it in front of them was dangerous. Then Tony added, "There was no cross up on the mountain when we went there on your graduation night."

"Oh, we got so drunk. You were a teaching assistant, I was a student. I know it wasn't professional to invite you up there with us, but we had a great time. We felt so lucky that you joined us!"

"Well, there wasn't that much of an age difference between us. I was twenty-nine, you were, what, twenty-two? Plus, you weren't in my class."

"I know," I said.

"But I knew exactly who you were."

I didn't know what to say. My heart was racing.

"Want to go up there, have a cigarette? It's such a beautiful night," he said. I nodded.

"To tell you the truth, I don't really feel like going home," I said. "Will your wife give you a hard time?"

"Forget her," he said, as he drove toward Mount Vodno.

After we pulled into the parking lot of the viewing platform, I stepped out of the car and walked, a little unsteadily, to the railing, from where there was a much better view of the city below. I was conscious of my slim figure, knowing how good I looked from behind. I slowed my pace, loosely swaying my hips. I could feel his eyes on me. I imagined him a beast of prey. My body tensed. The city was shrouded in smog. The pale light cast by the moon lent it a milky haze. The flickering lights of the cars and houses barely seeped through.

"It's a full moon," I pointed out, but as Tony didn't say a word, I went on talking. "So many lives, so many stories flow through the city, stories we'll never know," I said, wanting him to see that I was both tender and smart. "Yeah," he muttered and put his hands in his pockets. Then he rose slightly on his toes and settled back down on his heels.

"This is the exact same spot where we stood that night, at your graduation. Oh, how many years have passed . . ."

"Time flows like a river, but like stones we stay in place. And time erodes us without our realizing it," I said, quoting what my grandmother used to say when she'd had too much ouzo. Seeing he didn't know what to say, to provoke him, I said, "We've grown old."

"You haven't changed a bit," he said, turning toward me, resting an elbow on the railing. "You've always been beautiful. You still are."

I don't know how I found the courage to look him in the eyes. He was looking into mine too. He tapped his lips with his forefinger as a sign for me to kiss him. I leaned toward him and did as he asked. My mind raced with the thought that I was cheating on my husband for the first time and that I didn't give a damn. As my lips touched his, my mind went back to Marjan. I had lost my virginity to Marjan and whenever we had made love—something that lasted a long time—I would have two or three orgasms. But he left me after a few months, which really hurt. Boban I was in love with, but the sex was unfulfilling. Literally. All the magazines say that size doesn't matter, it's how you use it, which is what all my friends say, too. But even today, I'm embarrassed to admit that after all these years, I've been longing for something bigger, like Marjan's thing. I wanted to experience all those things that women bragged about on TV and in magazines, things I'd never had with Boban. Life with Boban was pleasant but dull, to the point that sometimes when I could see he wanted to make love, I took my time doing the dishes to avoid going to bed with him. So long, in fact, that in the end Boban often fell asleep. I felt bad about doing it, because Boban was always gentle with me. But I hated pretending that I enjoyed it. Once, Boban suggested we buy a dishwasher, but I told him I wouldn't hear of it, claiming that not only does it consume a lot of electricity, but it doesn't wash the dishes properly; things I knew weren't exactly true.

Tony's breath was warm and heavy, like his cologne. When our lips touched, he thrust his tongue into my mouth. It tasted bitter, like the cigarettes he smoked. He straightened up and tightened his grip around the waist. He was a head taller than me, so I had to crane my head back. His tongue rummaged around in my mouth as if in search of something. I wasn't sure I liked the way he kissed, but at least he did it passionately, something I hadn't experienced in what seemed like centuries. I responded in kind by thrusting my tongue into his mouth, our kisses turning into a battle of sorts. Our teeth clinked against each other, half my face was slimy with saliva. His hands ran down my back and squeezed both buttocks. He licked my chin and my throat and then his tongue found its way into my ear. "Sanya, Sanya," he murmured, groping me again. As he clutched me I felt something hard against my belly. I wasn't sure if it was his belt buckle or something else. He unbuttoned my blouse. He lifted one breast out of my bra and started licking and sucking it. "You're so beautiful," he whispered between kisses, which flattered me. It had been a long time since anyone had talked to me like that.

He took my arm and led me to the car. "Let's go somewhere else; it's too bright here," he said. I used my free hand to button up my blouse. "Don't," he said when we got back in the car. He took out my breast and sucked at it again. Then he turned the ignition on, put the car in gear, and drove away. So this is it, I thought to myself. This is what cheating is like. A car, darkness, alcohol. I was so glad I'd remembered to shave my armpits and wax my legs.

Tony drove slowly down the road. He turned off onto a dirt track, brought the car to a stop, then backed up, saying, "This isn't it." I wanted to ask him how he knew about these places, but decided not to. We drove a little further, then he turned down another dirt track that led to a small clearing with a large tree and bushes all around. He got out of the car and opened the back door, saying, "What are you waiting for?" He did it so fast it stunned me. "Come, it's roomier back here." It was so planned, so predictable, I was disappointed. The urge physically to cheat on my husband dwindled. But still I got in the back seat. I'd gone this far and there was no point in turning back.

Relax, I said to myself. Relax. Relax. That's what Marjan said the first few times we made love. Try to enjoy it, I said to myself. What you're doing isn't wrong. Everyone does it, even my supervisor, I said to myself as Tony licked my throat and breasts. I opened my eyes and watched him. Cupped in his hands, my breasts looked like teacups. He squeezed them. I let out a soft moan. Boban never squeezed me like this. He's much too gentle. He always treats me as if I were a doll. He lays me down and caresses me slowly, kissing me so gently it feels like butterflies fluttering over me. Tony tore off my pantyhose, pulled my underwear down, and lifted my skirt above my belly. I didn't quite know what was going on; he bit me, pinched me, and stuck his fingers in so hard it hurt. Then he stopped and unzipped his pants. He pulled them down around his knees. "Come on, just put it in your mouth a little," he said.

He was half-limp. He used one hand to yank it and the other to hold my head down near his groin. Then he put his penis in my mouth and jerked his hips back and forth. "Watch your teeth," he said, which was impossible to do because of his constant jerking. I felt like vomiting and my nose dribbled. I wanted to withdraw but he kept pulling my head down. I tried to be ladylike, not to grunt or snort, but it was impossible with his wild, jerky, increasingly desperate movements. He suddenly grew harder. This gave me hope, so I got into it a bit more. It was then I heard a long loud rumble in his belly. It sounded like distant thunder, but then it turned into a squeal. Almost instantly Tony stopped squirming and went limp. When he realized he'd gone soft, he started jerking himself off, trying to force my head back down, making me want to vomit. Then it happened again: a long, almost melodious squeal from his intestines, followed by a thick, rank smell that hit me full in the face. A wave of vomit rose in my throat and filled my mouth. I reached across Tony's lap toward the door handle, but couldn't open it in time. Chunks of pork liver, parsley, rakija, garlic sprayed the window and my hand with the wedding band.

"Christ!" Tony screamed. "What have you done? Get out of the way!" he said, shoving me aside as he squirmed out from under me with his pants down around his knees. He dragged himself over to the other side of the seat and kept as far away as possible from me. I opened the door. Crouched on my knees on the back seat, my head outside the car, I couldn't stop vomiting. Every time I thought I was done, I'd lift my head, straighten up, but then once again get a whiff of the smell that had hit me in the face and start retching and puking bile.

Tony didn't say a word or make a sound. It never occurred to me that he might feel sick too until I heard him whimpering and squirming in his seat. I turned and saw him hunched up, his head between his knees. He opened the door and tried to get out, forgetting that his pants were around his ankles. He fell with a dull thud beside the car and farted. God, I thought, it can't get any worse than this. But it did. Tony struggled to his feet and began to run, trying to pull his pants up as he did. With his spindly legs, he looked like a young stork learning to walk. He ran to the large tree and leaning against it, he started heaving with a low throaty sound, before letting out a short but powerful fart. Again and again he heaved, but nothing came up. Then he hid himself behind a bush. I heard more heaving. Though he was tall and the bush short, I couldn't see him. I stumbled toward the bush but a sharp smell hit me again, then Tony's garbled "Go away!"

As I stood there listening to him retch, sputter, groan, something glared in the corner of my eye. I turned and was blinded by a flashlight. A man approached in the darkness, shining the light in my eyes. Then he scanned my body with his flashlight. My blouse was undone, one breast was exposed, my skirt was askew.

"Good evening," said the policeman, coming up to me. "Is there a problem here?" I couldn't see his face. I prayed to God I didn't know him. It was then that Tony got up from behind the bush and stood beside me like a vanquished knight.

"What are you two doing here?" said the policeman. It was not a question so much as an accusation.

"We're having food poisoning," Tony said.

"You've been drinking," said the policeman, matter-of-factly.

"We had some pork liver," said Tony.

"We were at a restaurant," I added.

"Your IDs, please," said the policeman curtly. I longed to hear a hint of humanity in his voice.

"Just a second, just a second, they're in the car," said Tony, scurrying off to get them. I was repulsed by his submissiveness. But I followed behind, adjusting my skirt. The policeman stood over Tony as he opened the driver's door to get his license from the car. "What the fuck?" said the policeman, as he slipped in my vomit.

"Oh God, I'm so sorry," said Tony. "Don't ever eat at the Three Pheasants, you'll get food poisoning. I'll report them tomorrow. This sort of thing has never happened to me before,"

Tony was speaking anxiously, thrusting the license at the policeman, who was shining the torch on his shoe.

"Would you like a wet wipe?" I said, handing him the pack
I'd taken from my purse.

"I need to see your IDs," said the policeman, trying very hard
to maintain his composure, despite the vomit on his shoe.

I thought about telling him I didn't have my ID with me.
Just so he wouldn't see my surname. I was still half-blinded by
the flashlight, so I couldn't make out his face. I could tell he
was young, though, and my husband didn't mix much with the
young ones. Plus, the police force is a large organization, I reas-
sured myself. Maybe it wouldn't occur to him.

"You, too, ma'am," he said when he saw me clutching my
purse. I decided to show him my ID, knowing that if I didn't,
he could take me to the station, where things could get worse.

"Do you know what the penalty is for what you're doing?"
the policeman said, somewhat accusingly, as he checked Tony's
driver's license.

"For what?" Tony said. "Puking on Mount Vodno?"

"Shall I breathalyze you or are you going to carry on being a
smartass?" said the policeman, shining the light in Tony's eyes.
There was no logic to what he'd said, I thought to myself. Then
he flashed the light on my ID and fell silent.

"Spanakyoska," he said. "Spanakyoska." He flashed the torch
back in my face. And as he did so, I saw his lip curl into a smile.
*"The boss's wife is screwing some asshole, puking and shitting his guts
out on Mount Vodno,"* I imagined him telling his colleagues the
next day. *"And you should see the guy that's fucking the boss's wife.
He'd shit his pants. Literally! Ha, ha, ha!"* They were all going to
be laughing at my husband behind his back.

"Here," he said, handing our IDs back. "Don't let me catch you
here again. And don't eat at the Three Pheasants. My brother-in-
law got sick as a dog from eating kebabs there once." He turned
and vanished back into the darkness. Then we heard an engine
start. And even now, I don't know how it was that we didn't hear
him coming.

We got into the car. "Give me those wet wipes," said Tony, furiously wiping his face, his neck, and his hands. I tried to clean myself up too, but couldn't get the stench out of my nose. The smell of cologne and lavender had gone. He started the engine. The dashboard lit up and the radio came on, but all we heard was a crackling noise. The low-fuel indicator light was on. "Don't worry, we won't be stranded up here if I can help it," said Tony, trying to laugh things off, but at this point, nothing could possibly be funny.

I glanced at him now and then as he drove. What had I seen in him? I asked myself. In profile he looked more like a Neanderthal than ever. Even his hairstyle was ridiculous, as if his mother had put a bowl on his head and cut around the rim. His fingers were like sausages, unnaturally short in relation to his height. His torso was quite short, and with his spindly arms and round belly he looked like a spider. What on earth had come over me? I wondered. He's certainly no intellectual, I said to myself. After all these years at the institute, he hasn't done a stitch of research. He gets in on big international projects that never produce anything and ultimately prove pointless. I was filled with rage toward my supervisor and toward Irena, who I blamed the most for making me think I liked Tony, for making me think Tony liked me. No one had shown the slightest interest in me for a long time, I thought. I felt sorry for myself and my vision blurred from the tears welling up in my eyes. "When Boban finds out what I've done," I said to myself, my conscience burning with guilt, "he'll stop loving me." I wanted Tony to disappear. He couldn't hold a candle to Boban, my sweet love, my beloved husband, the love of my life.

We arrived at my apartment building. Tony turned toward me, glancing at my handbag. He played with the clip as he spoke: "This . . . you know . . . what happened tonight . . . it needs to stay here, between us." What a stupid ass, I thought. Does he really think I'm going to go around bragging about what a great lover he is?

"Tomorrow I'll call the restaurant. It was the liver."

Not until I'd stepped into the brightly lit lobby of our building did I realize I was covered with vomit and stank. I gingerly
entered our apartment. As luck would have it, Boban was asleep.

Rumena Bužarovska is one of the leading voices of contemporary short fiction in Macedonia. She has published three collections of short stories. Her stories "Waves" and "Lily" have appeared in *Best European Fiction 2016* and *Contemporary Macedonian Fiction*, respectively, both published by Dalkey Archive Press. She is Assistant Professor of American Literature at the University of Skopje.

Paul Filev is a freelance translator and editor. His translations from the Macedonian include *The Last Summer in the Old Bazaar* by Vera Buzarovska and *Alma Mahler* by Sasho Dimoski. He is the editor and translator of *Contemporary Macedonian Fiction* (Dalkey Archive Press 2019). He lives in Melbourne, Australia.